DIAMOND IN THE ROUGH

PART 2

Kamilah Haywood

DIAMOND IN THE ROUGH

PART 2

Kamilah Haywood

Toronto, Canada

Haywood, Kamilah, 1980-

ISBN-13: 978-0-9879195-4-0

Cover design Richie Dolo (@imautentik)

Founded in 2007, Kya Publishing is committed to the promotion and celebration of urban Canadian books, culture, and literacy.

© 2017 by Kya Publishing // KyaPublishing.com

Kya Publishing author, Toronto's Kamilah Haywood, has released the final edition of the trilogy: Diamond in the Rough – Part 2, a gritty tale about the injustices in the Canadian prison system.

After damaging her heart with the loss of her loved ones, and the subsequent loss off her mind, Diamond is falling victim to drugs to cope with her pain and has completely hit rock bottom. Everything that was her life is gone now, and Diamond has no interest in finding her way. She is dead walking around, having given up on life.

Diamond is quickly awakened when her rights as a prisoner are violated, and she has no choice but to fight. She meets Dr. Bakshi who opens her vision to a world she never knew existed.

It's survival of the fittest…but how fit is your survival when you're carrying the whole prison on your back, and you have the correctional department against you?

This book is dedicated to all the prisoners who have been lost and forgotten in the system: it's for the prisoners who have died in the system, or by the hands of the system. For the prisoners who have not awakened in the system, and are still lost to the system: this book is dedicated to you. For the families who have lost someone to the prison system: this is also dedicated to you.

"The walls, the bars, the guns, or the guards can never encircle or hold down the idea of the PEOPLE!"
~Huey P. Newton

R.I.P. Ashley Smith: this is in your honour.

RWAY4LIFE

CHAPTER ONE: Cloudy Days

***Like so many others will likely never leave this system,
and I ask you, Canada, how many must perish in a
federal prison before you demand change?***
~Nicole Kish

Time had frozen in all areas of my life. I mean, I didn't know who I was, or where I was going...in any direction. I was completely trapped in a revolving maze of the same reoccurring dream, and I could not wake up. I just lay there looking up into the darkness of blissful clouds of euphoria, waiting for my next fix—or should I say itch?—to awaken me to some part of myself. To actually be able to feel some sort of reality. To actually feel like I was present in this world or that I actually could participate in the day-to-day activities of my surroundings. I had to turn into a zombie to numb any sort of feeling I had, and I was digging...and digging...deeper, the more that time went on.

The darkness became a beauty, and I began to enjoy the beautiful creatures I was starting to see in the dungeons of the darkness. The bottomless pits were getting very deep and I was falling. I was starting to explore the intelligence they had and the beautiful conversations about living in the dark paths of life. My silence turned my ear and my ice cold, numb heart into a receiver for deep secrets. Some days I don't even think I realized all the information I was receiving: I just accepted it as it came and kept on moving. I was moving into an unknown path, but the future is always unknown...yet we continue to plan for a tomorrow that is never promised.

We spend every day of our lives in our minds, stressing over what tomorrow will bring and how hard we have to work for this to prepare for tomorrow. But what happens if you don't make it to that day? Then what? All this time we forget to enjoy right now and here.

I was not enjoying anything; I was completely stuck in last month's pain and last month's heroin hit, that I could not move at all. I just continued chasing the continuous high, hoping I would get the same feeling as the first time I tried it, only to realize I was becoming addicted. I don't think I even realized that. I was completely stuck. Erica told me after three days straight of using heroin you become an addict, but who was I to care or listen to her when she was using the same amount—if not more—than me?

The summer was hot and our room that we shared was even hotter. We barely ever left our room. Blonde would come upstairs to discuss business with Erica privately, and I would just act like I was sleeping because I did not want Blonde to know I was using heroin at the time. Here I was, this thug bitch who used to run and hustle drugs on the street, but now I was the one using the shit and turning into a client rather than a supplier. I had become the prey. I could not face anyone and let them know that on the outside world, so I completely blocked them out. I distanced myself from them entirely, and stopped making phone calls or even writing letters.

I would watch the mail come and not even open the envelopes. I would just pile the letters in drawer and leave them there for days, or until I was ready to explore those emotions.

I could not believe this shit. I mean you never get high on the drugs. *You never fuck with the drugs, period!* I could hear Jeru saying, but at this point, I did not give a fuck. I was so fucked up with everything going on like I said: I was not me. In fact, I did not know who I was or who I was becoming.

"I need another one. It's been too long and that limp bitch over there is sleeping. What are you waiting for you know where the stash is? Don't make me force you to do something you will regret. I already told you before: I control everything! Now go over there and get the bag before she wakes up!"

"COUNT!"

Once again I was saved by the bell. Shine was driving me crazy, always trying to get me to violate the prison codes. I was no damn cell rat and I was definitely no thief. I could hear the stomping of the guards coming up the stairs in our house, and I made my way quickly to cover Erica up as she highly slept in her heroin bliss. I quickly stood up for the count, and of course it was fat-ass Melissa who was looking in the little glass window of our room.

"Where is Erica?"

"She's sleeping?"

"She knows she has to be up for count!"

"I'll let it slide this time, but next time I won't be so nice, Brown!"

I did not even bother to respond because I knew any wrong move…and our room would have heat. That was no good right now, seeing as we were both high on heroin. The guards quickly made their way out of our house, after completing the count, and I knew we had the rest of the night to enjoy getting high. We could miss the days going by without a care in the fucking world because we had a bag full with an ounce of heroin to get us through.

I tried to clean up a bit and organize the room when I heard Erica shuffling around—I knew that meant she was about to get up from the heroin nap she had fallen into after her hit. She continued rolling around in the bed until she uncovered her face to notice me cleaning up our room.

"Hey! You ok?"

"Ya, jus' cleanin' up shit."

"Coppers came by already?"

"Ye!"

"Shit, an' you let me sleep?"

"It's aiight, I handled it."

"Ok! You shoulda grabbed my stash!"

"I don't touch shit dat ain't mine."

"Listen we good! I vibe you or I wouldn't be kickin' it wit you. I don't jus' kick it wit anyone. I mean, let me say this right. See the first day we came?"

"Ye?"

"Well, I got so mad because I didn't wanna share a room with you because I thought you were cute."

"What?" Did this bitch just say she thought I was cute?

"Never mind."

"No, I didn't hear you!"

"I said I thought you were cute, and I have a man on the outside but I haven't been really calling him because I found out he's been fuckin' around and shit. I'm kinda into you."

I paused. I had to process this shit. Did this girl just say she liked me? I had a warm feeling inside. It was weird. I thought she was attractive, but I really didn't know the feelings or where they came from. I mean, I always knew something inside of me was missing…but was this it? I knew from the first time I laid eyes on this girl that I couldn't stop watching her, but was it an attraction…or was it just the drugs?

"Ok. Well, um. Ok. I'm gonna finish cleaning then take a shower."

"You want another hit?"

"Nah. You want some breakfast?"

"Maybe later?"

"Ok cool!"

I got myself together and headed for the shower; I had to process this, but I looked back at Erica and could see the disappointment. Her grey eyes had gone to dark green and were now filled with sorrow. I was not sure if she felt that I rejected her.

My shower was long, and the water was so soothing I could feel the little droplets of water bouncing off my skin like a tropical rain forest shower. Everything is such a blissful moment when you're high. I mean everything. I needed to climb higher. I could start to feel the cravings coming on; the cravings are a bitch. The crash, the jones, whatever the fuck you wanna call it. That shit is what made people go crazy and fuck up their lives trying to get a next fix. The jones is real and it's unbearable. It's so unbearable that you would leave your own newborn baby starving to get that fix if you needed to.

I exited the shower and made my way back to our room to find that Erica was gone. I got dressed quickly and made my way downstairs to look for her, but she was nowhere to be found. I went back upstairs to our room...but she was not there either. I decided I could either sit there and jones for a hit...or face the feelings that Erica had brought to my attention, to get my mind in another place.

I realized there was some type of attraction between us. I was not sure how deep it was yet, but there was definitely a connection and I did not want it to go away. I wanted to keep her close. I decided to write a little letter and leave it on her bed. I wanted it to be sweet but meaningful; I wanted her to know I felt what she felt. I felt four words would be enough. I first thought of Aaliyah's four page letter and I thought: I'll just do four words.

Erica,
I feel the same.
D

I placed the letter gently on her pillow and made my way back downstairs towards the kitchen only to find Erica sitting on the couch watching TV in a dark green robe. I could have sworn I just went down there and she was not there. She did not look in my direction but she immediately went upstairs when she realized I was downstairs. I continued my way into the kitchen to proceed to make myself breakfast.

The kitchen units in the medium section of Grand Valley's prison were very simple. The houses looked more like cottage homes, or I guess you could say cabins. Our kitchen had brown wooden cupboards with beige kitchen tiles to match. There was a window looking out the kitchen to see the compound of the other cabins, and a backdoor for the guards to enter the unit. I tell you, anything to make your stay here as depressing as possible, but I guess that's a part of rehabilitation. It was definitely not the Marriott.

I quickly made some toast with peanut butter and jam, then made my way back to our room. I did not want to be down there. There was an eerie feeling about the downstairs, although I couldn't put my finger on what it was just yet. I still had yet to come across the other ladies who were staying in the house, and I really was not interested in making may any new "friends." Ain't no friends in prison.

I made my way back upstairs to find Erica in her bed with her back turned facing the wall. She did not look at me or say a word, but I noticed the letter I left was gone so I knew she had read it. I ate my toast quietly and remained silent until she decided to speak.

"You want another hit?"

"Ye! Let me finish my food first, though. You don't wanna eat?"

"No, not yet. I'm gonna get you to hold this bag for me though so I'm not always in it. This has to last us until the next shipment of girls come. I have another girl coming with another package from the West and that's the mother load. That package will last us for a long time."

"Aiight, no problem."

"I like your vibe. You're quiet, and you're chill."

"Thanks. I like your vibe too."
"You finished your toast yet?"
"Ye."
"Come, let's go to the bathroom."

CHAPTER TWO: Pretty Eyes

Open your eyes; look within.
Are you satisfied with the life you're living?
~Bob Marley

Her eyes were beautiful. I sat there looking into the windows of her soul, but the depth of her darkness was endless. I could not get a feel for any light or love at all. The deeper I looked, the darker her eyes got, and I was so high that I kept on searching for that one touch of love that was not there. The more she kissed my soul with her precious lips as our bodies embraced in a cosmic chemistry, the deeper I danced with a demon. The more I opened my soul and bonded to this forbidden dance with the devil, the more she took pieces of my innocent soul.

She kissed my neck gently and pushed her forbidden love inside my chest. Her touch was venom, yet I craved every moment. I was passionately clawing my fingers down her back as she smiled, and I thought I saw fangs.

I quickly pushed her off me. "What the FUCK, man?"

"What?"

"Yo, man, don't touch me!"

"What is your problem? Like, did I do something wrong?"

"Nah yo. You're jus on some evil shit yo!"

"It's the drugs. It can do that to you. It plays tricks wit your mind, baby."

"Nah yo. You had fangs!"

"What? Diamond you're crazy!"

"Nah yo!"

"Diamond, like, teeth fangs? Like vampire shit?"

"Ye Yo! You on some next shit yo!"

"Diamond your jus' high man. You need to come down a bit," she said, and started laughing.

"Shit ain't funny!"

"Calm down! I'm going to get my girl and get you some brew. She's been workin' on it for a minute. It should be ready now."

"What the fuck is brew?"

"It's prison-made alcohol."

"I'll introduce you to her. She's good people. We call her Tatts. She does work for everyone in here so if you want one just let me know. I'll give her some dope and she'll fix you up."

"Ok."

Erica left the room and I stayed in my bed. My head was spinning all over the place and I started to see images coming out of the wall. Little faces of people. I was fuckin' tripping. I was so high, and I had been up for too many days. I think in total I had been up for five or six days and I could not put my finger on it. All I knew was if I did not sleep I would fuckin' knock someone the fuck out or I was going to end up in segregation and put the whole house on lockdown 'cause I got caught. That's some real heat score shit.

Erica came back quickly with a big two liter Sprite bottle hidden in her green robe, and some white girl that looked like she was in a heavy metal band or some shit. She had long, dark, black, hair and tattoos all over her arms. She was dressed in an all black t-shirt with all black pants and all black boots. She was tall and looked like she could knock somebody the fuck out if they fucked with her. Erica handed me the pop bottle and ordered me to guzzle it while she dealt with Tatts, giving her some dope to send her on her way.

By the time I got through half the bottle of guzzling, I was drunk. That shit was strong as a muthafucka. It was like hard liquor times ten. Now I was starting to feel "normal." That sketchy shit was starting to go away, and I was getting tired. My eyes were starting to close as Erica rubbed my back to sleep and before I knew it...lights out.

I was not sure how long, or if I had fallen asleep for long at all. All I knew was when I opened my eyes in the dark hours of the night, Erica was nowhere to be found. I was very weak and frustrated all together—I wanted to move, but I could not. I stayed in my bed thinking of what tomorrow would bring...only to realize I was stuck behind these prison walls with no escape. The thought alone was tormenting! I started to think of my family and how I could not see or reach them at all. I thought about how Xavier and Jeru were dead. I could see their faces in my head but I could never talk to them again: it was my choices that lead them to their death, and I had to live with this shit. All this fuckin' thinking. FUCK! I rolled over to the corner of my bed by the wall, grabbed the half a bottle of the brew I had left, and started guzzling it down. In one long gulp the bottle was done and I lit a cigarette. It was frustrating, and all these feelings were coming up that I did not want to deal with. I needed more drugs. Where the fuck was Erica? Oh shit yeah! She gave me the stash.

I quickly made my way to the bathroom and just as I was about to open the door someone pushed the door closed. I tried to open it again but they pushed it closed again. FUCK man! I just want to do a hit. I went back in my room because there was no fuckin' way I could be a heat score. As I tried to quickly make my way across the hall I heard the door being opened—I turned back to see who it was, and it was Fatback.

"Yo girl!" she whispered.

"What's up?"

"She's out like a fuckin' light again. Gonna carry her in the room in a minute."

"Ok." I whispered back.

I made my way back to the room and waited for Fatback to come back with Erica. It did not take her long to drag Erica's dead weight across the hallway back to our room. She was making little heaving noises as if she was coming back to life or if she was going to vomit. Fatback struggled to put her limp body on the bed, and I tried my best to assist her with the strength that I had.

"Take care of her! She's blacked out again. She don't fuckin' listen an' is always doin' more than she can handle," Fatback said.

I grabbed the dark, grey metal garbage bucket that we had in the corner of our room by the T.V stand. I put it by Erica's head in case she needed to lean over and vomit. I knew it was coming. Fatback was rocking side to side trying to keep her eyes open but I knew she was high also and needed to get back to her room and lay down.

"It's ok I got her."

"You sure?"

"Ya. You go back to your room. I will take care of her until she is ok" I said.

Fatback slowly stumbled out our room and I could hear her heavy footsteps down the hallway before she closed her bedroom door at the end of the hallway. I sat at the edge of my bed as I watched Erica. Waiting and thinking on what my next move should be. I was jonesin' but I also wondered if I should wait to see if she vomited, or if I should run to the bathroom and quickly get a next hit. Erica was quiet and she was not moving so I decided to quickly run to the washroom and do my shit. I couldn't wait any longer. The itch was coming on too strong and the more I waited, the more I wanted to scratch the fuck out of my skin. I started to think morbid thoughts of doing things in the room and that was just a complete heat score. I knew the rules, and I knew I could not risk getting caught.

I quickly and quietly made my way to the bathroom, closed the door, and handled my business. I made sure this time when I did my hit it was a big one to last me a long time so I would not have to have the feeling of jonesin' for a long time. I could not handle that feeling at all. I sat back on my bed with the package carefully stuffed and secured in my bra, and watched Erica to see if she had moved…but she had not. I was able to do everything I needed to do and get back to acting as if nothing had happened.

I was starting to go back into my cloud of bliss when Erica started heaving again. She quickly turned over her body with the minimal strength she had. I could see her body was starting to convulse, so I quickly grabbed the garbage just before I saw the vomit fly out of her mouth. It was a clear, watery, substance that smelled like sour orange juice. It was gross. As I was holding the garbage can, Erica's eyes popped out her head and her veins in her forehead danced from side to side, I could not help but wonder if I was in a dream? The moment felt like it had already happened in another life. I felt like I had met Erica before but I just did not know from where.

"FUUUUUCK!" Erica belted out as her body continued to dry heave, but no liquid was coming out of her mouth.

"You alright?" I asked. She gave me the evilest look as if I was not supposed to be talking, because I was making it worse. I realized it was best for me to just keep my mouth closed. I continued to hold the pail underneath Erica's mouth until she motioned with her hand that she was done. Erica plopped her body back on the bed and curled into a ball. She began closing her eyes and I knew it was best for me to clean up the evidence before the guards came around. I quickly made my way into the washroom with the garbage bucket, emptied its contents in the toilet, and flushed it down the drain. I started spraying the garbage bucket out when I heard someone knocking on the door…good thing I locked the door!

"Just give me second!" I said as I continued to clean out the garbage bucket.

"Hurry the fuck up, other people need to use the washroom!" I was not sure who the voice was, but it was unfamiliar.

"I said hold on!"

"And I said hurry the fuck up!"

I was getting pissed off at this point because one, the person was being disrespectful and two, this person had no patience. I continued cleaning the garbage bucket and started to dry it out with paper towel that was also located on top of the bathroom counter, when this bitch started getting really out of hand. The bathroom door was locked and the person on the other side of the door tried to open it.

"I said hold on!"

"AND I SAID HURRY THE FUCK UP!"

It was at that moment I realized I was dealing with an irrational, disrespectful individual that was not going to listen to anything I had to say. There was no way in reasoning or discussing anything with this person at this point. I had to fight. I never took disrespect from anyone anyway. I was high as a fuckin' kite and I was floating on the clouds; I did not even want to fight, but I had no choice. The disrespect this bitch was giving, I had to put her in her place and quickly.

I quickly opened the bathroom door and before the bitch could even speak, I smashed the metal garbage bucket in her mouth. She stumbled back towards my bedroom door and tried to gain her balance, but before she could react, I swung my left fist across her jaw. The whole house must have heard the commotion because everyone came out their rooms from downstairs and upstairs to run and watch. Blonde tried to stop us from fighting, but Fatback quickly told her no. I jumped up in the air while kicking the tall, brown skin girl with glasses and curly, red hair in her stomach. She did not have chance. She started grabbing her stomach and that's when I gave her the final blow. A hard, right uppercut, then a one left to her head. She quickly fell into a sitting position and I saw Erica standing in our doorway, watching and smiling. Blonde lunged towards me in front of the doorway of the bathroom and held me back.

"That's fuckin' enough! Everyone go back to their rooms and pick this fuckin' drama queen up off the fuckin' floor! Holy fuck! You alright?" she said to me as she rubbed the top of my head, smiling.

"Ya."

"You're a quiet one for a reason! I see that now. You don't like to be bothered. I got you. No one will bother you right, Erica and Fatback?" she said as Erica and Fatback stood listening.

"Damn right. She's a little solider. Young, but we'll show her the way! I saw that uppercut you got. Christ. You in boxin'?" Fatback said.

"No." I said.

"She sum quiet bitch ain't she?" Fatback said.

They all focused in on me, getting me all uncomfortable. I was also embarrassed because I hated having to fight anyone. I was use to drinking and not giving a fuck but let me be straight: I was a lover. I was never a fighter and this heroin shit did not make me want to fight anyone.

"It's the quiet ones you gotta watch!" Erica said.

"Let's call it a night. We know what's good." Blonde said.

Everyone was gone out of sight. I couldn't help but notice the shimmering gloss in Erica's eyes as she kept smiling at me. She walked in our room first, and turned back at me to smile. Her eyes were different. They had a way of pulling me in. They were pretty, but there was something else that was calling me. I just didn't know what it was yet.

"I really like you Diamond! You're different than anyone I have ever met."

CHAPTER THREE: Isolation

*Freedom is not worth having if it does not include the
freedom to make mistakes.
~Ghandi*

About a month had gone by and I was really getting comfortable with my sentence. I was high all the time. The mother package of shipments made its arrival from the West Detention Centre, so we were all stacked for goods. I mean we had kush, crack, cocaine, heroin, and perks. There was one girl that brought the package for Erica, and another girl Fatback had robbed in the bathroom of House Three, which was considered the house no one ever wanted to live in. It was full of informants, and people that hurt children or killed them. Somehow Fatback got in the house and held the girl hostage after she arrived in the bathroom. She went inside her pussy and took out the package: it was full of crack/cocaine and heroin. The girl knew she could not inform or she would be fucked for bringing in the package in the first place. Plus she would get terrorized for the rest of her stay for being an informant and ratting out Fatback who was one of the women that had the most respect in the prison, alongside Blonde and Erica. Silence was her only option and she knew that or there would be huge consequences for opening her mouth. Instead she let Fatback have her way, and in turn became one of Fatback's clients to buy some of her own drugs back for personal use. Ain't that a bitch!

It had been a while since I had called or reached out to my family, and I knew they were worried about me. The letters I was receiving had started to increase, so I decided it was best for me to give my house a call to let them know I was ok. I did not know what I would say or how I would say it. The best thing for me to do—like I always did—was just jump in and get it done.

"Hello," I said in a whisper.

"Who is this? I can barely hear you." It was my Mother. I was happy to hear her voice, a familiar voice. It had been a while.

"It's me, Diamond."

"Diamond?" She said.

We both sat in silence for a moment, neither of us knowing who should proceed first until I decided to continue the conversation. I knew she was hurt because of how I just left her. I was not really abandoning her though, I just did not know how to feel. It was too much for me to deal with my family and do my time at the same time.

"How you been?"

"Same old shit! Where have you been? How come you have not called in over a month?"

"I've just been doing my time."

"Really? That's all you have to say, Diamond?"

"What else do you want me to say? You want me to lie to you and make up some bullshit story that's not true?"

"No. So when can we come see you?"

"I'm not sure yet. I think I gotta get on some application and then you guys can apply."

"Did you get it yet?"

"No."

"Well what are you waiting for?"

"Nothing."

"You seem different, Diamond. You sound different. You sound very distant. Why do you sound like that?"

"Someone has to use the phone," I lied.

"So what does that mean?"

"I have to go."

"Ok."

"Tell everyone I said, Hello!"

"I will. Take care Diamond."

"You too." I was cold and distant as I hung up the telephone receiver.

I could not feel or express any emotion. My mind was gone. My heart was frozen and all that mattered was getting high to numb the pain that I was feeling deep inside my heart. No one was waiting to use the telephone. I lied to my Mother. I was pushing the world I knew the most away, to throw myself into a world that I did not know at all. I sat there in the chair looking out the window at the prison fence that surrounded the jail. Thoughts of escaping kept entering my mind. I wondered how the fuck was I going to make it out of here.

"You dumb bitch! Quit sitting here like a baby and go upstairs and get more drugs. You always have to sulk around like a God damn suck! Don't make me fuckin' hurt you. I'm not in the mood today Diamond—remember what fuckin' happened the last time?" Shine said while slapping me in the head.

"Smarten up! Don't fuckin' make me create a scene. You fuckin' obey my orders. I run the fuckin' show. I'm sick and tired of you lame ass bitches fuckin' actin' like you have any say!"

I turned to look around to make sure no one was watching, made my way upstairs quietly, and I could hear Shine mumbling something but I was not sure what. I got inside our room and of course Erica was passed out. It was too early for her to be up. I decided to get my day going by doing a couple of lines in the washroom and then heading to the building for my appointment with Case Management. I also wanted to find out about visitation. I quickly made my way into the washroom again to do a couple more lines to keep me from getting sick. I hid the package securely in our stash spot, and made my way over to Case Management.

It was a Wednesday morning and of course most of the prison women were out doing their prison jobs. The compound was full of people exercising, hanging out, and working. I did not speak to anyone or acknowledge anyone either. I just quickly made my way into the building; I could see the other woman watching me but I did not even give them a second glance.

I arrived in the main building for my appointment with my caseworker who would be managing my case while I had my stay at Grand Valley. I sat at the front of the building waiting; there was a lot of traffic at that part of the building. They had school programs, workshops, cleaning, hair school, canteen stores, and also a place where you could receive incoming calls. I sat there for about twenty minutes before some short, brown haired lady with glasses that was limping a bit came out. She had a on a red, v-neck sweater and some blue jeans with brown shoes. She did not smile with me at all; she just opened the door and proceeded to walk down the hall towards her office. Without a word, I followed her down the hall. I was not going to speak until she spoke.

We arrived at her office which was impeccably organized. There was not a paper or a pen out of place. Her office smelled fresh and I knew she meant business. She did not ask me to sit, but I sat anyway, making myself comfortable. She did not look impressed.

"The reason I've called you down here, Miss Brown, is because I'm hearing some things on the compound about your house. I was wondering if you would be kind enough to help me with some information?"

"What is it you're hearing?"

"There was a robbery that took place in House Three. One of the women in your house did the robbery and took a bunch of drugs. Would you know anything about that?"

"No. Never heard anything about that."

"Hmmm," she said, trying to look in my eyes.

I did not look away. I realized now this women was not my caseworker. She was the Warden and she thought I was a rat. Little did she know, I did not operate that way. Whatever I knew, I never told anyone. Period. I knew the prison code and it could cost you your life.

"Ok Mrs. Brown, if that is how you are going to play it."

"Play what?"

"Those who don't cooperate with staff here at Grand Valley have repercussions to their actions. So you will learn the hard way."

"I don't know what you're talking about."

"Please let yourself out!"

I got up and walked as calmly as I could out the main building. There were cameras everywhere. I could not make one wrong move, but I had let Erica, Fatback and Blonde know what was going on. Lauren the Warden was onto us and either the dogs were coming, or the guards were going to do a raid. Either way, we needed to be prepared.

I got inside the house and immediately ran to Blonde's room. She was the one who was most responsible and sober, so I decided I had to warn her first. I knocked on her door.

"Who's dat?"

"It's me, Dee?"

"What's good girl? I'm trying to sleep!"

"Need to talk to you now!"

"Hold on, give me a sec."

I was pacing back and forth in a panic. I just wanted to get everyone on board so we were good. Blonde opened the door in one mint lime green house coat and yellow bandana. I wanted to laugh but I knew now was not the time.

"What's up girl? I was just dreaming about my man. So dis shit better be good."

"Yo! I got called over to the building because they said I had a case management meeting. I got a letter."

"That's normal we all get that shit when we first come."

"No listen. It was Lauren. Bitch pulled me in her office. Asking bout Fats move."

"What you say?"

"Nothing."

"What she say?"

"Told me I'd learn the hard way."

"FUUUCK MAN! Dese muthafuckas is comin'!"

"Exactly what I thought!"

"Fuck! Everybody gotta get up, NOW! House has to be set. Drugs gotta be hooped. We have to put everything in order. There's gonna be a raid or dogs. Wake everyone up!"

I ran upstairs and banged on everyone's door— Blonde did the downstairs. Everyone was pissed off, but once they heard Blonde cussing everyone they knew what was up. All Blonde kept yelling was: "6 UP". Everyone started running all over the place. Hiding shit. I was in my room with Erica, and told her everything that happened. She said they would probably try to come and piss test me, or anyone from the house, to see if there were drugs in the house or if anyone was using. Naturally, everyone was paranoid. We were prepared now, and just waiting for them to make their first strike.

It did not take long before two guards came to grab me for a piss test like Erica said. I sat in the all-white isolation unit for two hours, and I did not pee. I would not pee. Peeing would only let the guards know that we had drugs in our house. Instead I took an institutional charge and two days in segregation. I had no packages on me, because we knew that was probably going to be their first strike, so we prepared for that and moved the package to the least suspected person in the house which was the bitch I beat up the other day. She wanted to earn some respect so she did the job no problem. Plus, they would least suspect her because she was a model prison inmate. Erica talked her into it, and it worked. I had to spend the weekend in isolation and it was the worst ever. I was going through the worst withdrawal of heroin possible. I did not eat. I did not sleep. All I did was vomit, diarrhea, sweat, and shake. I tried to hide it from the guards because I was on camera, but it was the hardest thing I could do.

One late night or very early morning, I heard the dogs coming in the prison and I knew that's when the house was being raided. It was the last day in segregation for me and I knew they would hit the house without me being there because it was the smartest thing to do. A double hit. They would think the women would never expect it, but Erica was fuckin' smart. She said she knew all about the Warden and her plans of strategy. She said they had a history from Prison for Women days. Erica knew exactly how this woman operated and she had a problem with Erica, Fatback, and Blonde because she knew them from those days before Prison for Women closed down and Grand Valley opened. This wasn't about anyone else. This was personal.

Erica said Lauren was going to brutalize anyone who was in the way to get to Erica. She would, one by one, strip them away until Erica was alone. She said it was best that I stay away from her, but I did not listen. I did not realize it then, but that was the worst choice I could have possibly made...but I was a fighter. I did not back down from anyone, but sometimes you have to realize when you're fighting a fight you can't win.

It did not take long before they came again. It was the early morning to catch me off guard. I remember just turning over to try to get a good rest which had not been possible in a long while, when I heard my cell being unlocked. There were six guards and fat ass Melissa leading the way. I stood up to face them thinking they were bringing me back to House Five, but the truth is they had another plan for me.

"Get organized, Brown! You're going to maximum security!"

"What are you talkin' about? WHAT THE FUCK YOU MEAN MAX?" I said in utter disbelief. *"You're going to continue your stay in maximum security! Now we can do this easy or we can do it hard. It's your choice, but we won't be taking all day while you decide."* I started tuning out the fat bitch and zoning my vision on the other guards as they positioned. I realized either way they were going to fight me to take me, so I wouldn't go down without a fight. I rushed towards the cell door while Melissa was still talking, and jump-kicked her in her chest, causing her to fall back on the other guards. I knew they could not carry her weight so that would give me an advantage for a moment to attack her and do some damage before they took me down.

I started punching her repeatedly in her face until I broke her nose and caused massive blood to spill. The guards behind her pulled her back and rushed me to the ground. The amount of kicks and punches I felt all over my body caused me to start seeing stars as my vision went blurry. I felt one boot in my face from one of the officers, and the blows were enough to knock me out. Everything went black and I could hear Melissa calling me a "fuckin' bitch" repeatedly. It was then, while taking my last breath, that I remembered as painful as it was that I had knocked out completely.

CHAPTER FOUR: Maximum

*There will be no prison which can
hold down our movement.*
~Huey P. Newton

The coldness that I rested my head on was colder than a winter's night in the Toronto streets. I slowly opened my eyes to the darkness that surrounded me; the pain immediately throbbed all over my body as I tried to move, but I could not move. It was way too excruciating and the more I moved, the more the pain throbbed. I tried to move my hand to feel my face but I was shackled with handcuffs from my hands to my feet. The concrete floor was getting colder as my mind started to race, and I began to panic.

"SOMEBODY LET ME THE FUCK OUT!" I screamed at the top of my lungs, hearing my voice echoing in the silence.

"HELP ME! SOMEBODY!" I wanted to cry, but my anger would not let me.

"Listen you stupid weak bitch! You got us in here and your chants of agony will not get us out! Now shut-up and deal with the fuckin' shit you got us in before you bring the pigs back here for more and you have to hide like a little punk while I fight them. You don't know what you have done. They wheelchaired you over here in a straightjacket while constantly beating you, until they threw you in the cell on the floor and handcuffed you. I had to take those beatings and fight them the whole way because your punk ass ran as soon as you hit the bitch."

"Just shut-up shut-up shut-up..." I couldn't handle Shine and her mouth right now. Always blaming me when it was her who got us in all this bullshit in the first place. As I began to shut Shine up—or so I thought—I heard my cell door being opened and the light in my cell was turned on. From where? I didn't know, but I would figure all that out. My eyes closed shut from the brightness as my cell door was being opened. I could hear the keys dangling as it was being unlocked, and male voices talking, but I could not make out what they were saying. I continued to lie on the cold concrete floor playing lifeless in anticipation of what was next to come. I also hoped that they did not hear me telling Shine to shut-up, but of course my luck ran out, so hoping was not the best option for me.

The cell door opened, and I could hear the officers walking in my space. I wanted to move, but I continued playing lifeless.

"HELLO THERE! You awake? Think this stinky bitch needs a shower, don't you?" The officer said while laughing.

"Hell ya she does! Let's give her a shower!" the other male officer said. I was in no position to get up and have a shower. I could barely move.

"Hey, you! Get up, sleepy time is over," the leading officer said. He started to kick my body to try and get a response. First the kicks were gentle, then they got harder as each kick passed. I couldn't handle it, so I cried out in agony.

"STOOOOOOP!" I belted out with all the energy I had.

"There we go, she's alive!" he said laughing with the other officer.

His accent was British, but a bit faded. I could tell because he sounds like some family members from my Mother's side of the family who sounded the same.

"It's time to have a shower!" he said laughing again. Before I could even try to open my eyes I felt the presence of him standing over me, laughing in my face.

"Go go!" he said.

Just as I was about to open my eyes, I felt a big cold splash of water cover my body. I wanted to scream and move but there was no energy. I could feel the tears of pain coming from my throat and then another bucket of water got thrown on me again. The water was freezing cold like there were ice cubes also being thrown along with it.

"That should do her for a good shower," he laughed.

I began to shiver, and the sores on my body screamed in pain. I started to open my eyes to the light—as hard as it was, I had to do it. I needed to see the face of the bastard that was doing this to me. I forced through the pain to open one of my eyes and I saw a glimpse of him. He was tall, slender, with a dark brown buzz cut and glasses. I remember his boots because he had red lips kissing on the side of his boots. He must have got a sticker or some shit to have it on there. I would never forget what I could make out of him because one day I would get him for this. The officers began to exit the cell, and I felt the light go out again.

I burst into tears, not because of the water but because of the fact that I was restrained and I could not get out of it to fight back or even move around in my cell if I wanted to. The officers left me there to shiver. The coldness was so cold that I could feel it going into my bones. I felt like I was frozen, but it was helping my wounds in an awkward way. It was like my body was becoming numb. I started to drift into the darkness of the silent cold bitterness that I was laying in…a dark cloud that was pulling me into the night's drift. Was it even night? I did not know, because I was just existing in this world. A speck of life no one knew, so my death would not matter as I drifted into the dark concrete stillness that was so comforting, yet forbidden.

It was not long until I was awaken by the sounds of a soothing female voice. The voice was so unfamiliar that I thought I was dreaming.

"Hello! Miss Brown, are you ok? Can you open your eyes and see my two fingers?" This voice was so comforting that I wanted to follow the sound. My eyes forced opened but my vision was blurry.

"Hi there. We are going to get you all better. Can you take the cuffs off please?" she said.

"We had to make sure she was not going to injure herself or other officers," the same British accent responded.

"Take them off! She is not going to injure anyone in this position and after you remove them excuse yourself! I am going to interview the inmate and see what path of rehabilitation needs to be taken."

"Your call, Dr. Bakshi!" the British male spoke.

I could hear him searching for the key when I felt a warm, soft, hand embrace my forehead.

"My gosh! She's freezing and her clothes are soaking wet! What the hell happened here?"

"I don't know. I'm not sure," the officer mumbled.

"Weren't you the officer on site? It does not matter anyway. ARE YOU OK?" The soothing soft voice asked.

I opened my one eye and I swear I saw an angel. She had this beautiful shimmering, brown skin with long dark black hair. Her eyes went into my soul and I felt love. She had a glow of light around her, and the energy gave me strength. I opened my other eye and she smiled. "Are you ok Miss Brown? Wink once if you need the hospital. Wink twice if you need just my assistance. My name is Dr. Bakshi, and I am the prison physician. I'm here to help you." She turned and darkness started to fill the cell.

"Take the cuffs off officer, and excuse us!" she said firmly but there was rage behind her tone.

I could hear it. Reminded me of my Mother when she tried to control her anger but she was pissed at something I did. The thought made me laugh and I could not help but start laughing. The pain stopped for a minute and I felt joy. I felt home. I missed home.

"Weakness, you silly bitch!" Of course Shine has to always spoil the moment.

My hands were finally free and with the help of Dr. Bakshi, she lifted me slowly up on the cot in my cell. The officer was still watching, but neither of us paid him any attention, as he exited the cell. I felt a sense of comfort with her.

"Lay down. I know you're in pain. I'm going to give you something to relax your body so your mind is not going crazy." Little did she know there were all kinds of conversations and fights going on in my mind, especially between Shine and me.

"Don't trust this bitch, she's just like them. She's a pig!" I ignored Shine and listened to what Dr. Bakshi had to say.

"I need to understand why you reacted the way you did. You're a baby in here. You need to go home to your family, and fighting officers and injuring them is not the way. That will get you killed. You are just another number to them, but you must have a powerful mind and spirit to conquer them…and I don't mean with your fists either. They outnumber you. So please tell me the best you can, with the energy you have, what happened?"

Anytime someone asked me too many questions, I didn't trust them. She was on their side.

"I don't know," I said in a whisper.

"I'm not going to pressure you for the story. It's the past, and we are here now, so how do we pass this? I will help you, but you have to help yourself. The police are coming to charge you and you will have to do video court. Best thing is to plea because they have you on camera hitting Melissa. We can get you fixed from there. This is not the first time this has happened and won't be the last. You have to be smarter than them to beat them and this is not the way." Something made me know she was right but I just remained quiet and listened. Why was this woman giving me all this information? Made me wonder if she was working for them on some good cop, bad cop shit.

CHAPTER FIVE: Rehabilitation

Prison is about making money,
not about rehabilitation.
~Kamilah Haywood

I didn't know how many weeks it was, until I woke up with energy to finally move around. Dr. Bakshi had been coming every day to visit and give me morphine to get through the pain. I had judged her wrong. She really was a good person. It was like I had been sent this angel from a higher power to get me through my time. She always had the right words to calm me down, but I was sure the morphine was helping with that also. She was a beautiful Indian woman with nice, smooth brown skin. She had light brown hazel eyes and straight white teeth that she took good care of. She always smelled good and I knew she liked wearing name brand scents like my Mother. Some of the smells seemed familiar. She reminded me of a girl I went to school with in elementary school around Roche Court days, when I was five years old. She had that transparent spirit that you couldn't resist because it helped give you light in your dark tunnel. Dr. Bakshi was that light, showing me the way out of this mess. She talked to me about things that I had never heard of before like spirituality, meditation, prayer, and reading.

I loved reading but had not read in so long. She got me to expose that I was a good poet in my younger days, but got caught up with the streets and lost my passion for anything but money. Dr. Bakshi got me to pay attention to myself and she always kept telling me that I needed to go inside of myself and connect with my soul. At first I thought she was crazy, but eventually I realized she was not, and when she left I would yearn to learn more.

I started to move around my cell a bit to try and get things organized, once I had my strength back. I was also able to see Fat Melissa who had a vendetta against me because of what I did to her nose. I listened to Dr. Bakshi's advice, and ignored her even though she did very disrespectful things at times. She would throw my food in my cell, and not respond to questions I asked, but I could not engage in what she was trying to get me to do. She wanted me to react for a chance to abuse me again. I had enough problems on my plate and I could not allow Melissa to be one of them.

It was early morning and I just received my breakfast: some bullshit slop they called porridge. I was waiting for my canteen order so I could get my snacks and hygiene products. I had already received my belongings so it was not long for the others things to arrive. I had started reading this book Dr. Bakshi had given me called *The Autobiography of a Yogi*. It was really interesting and had started to open my eyes to more than just life on this physical earth. She has also brought me books on meditation and practices of yoga and Tai Chi.

I had a lot to do with my days. I would eat breakfast, have morning meditation, and then yoga. After that it was lunch time so I would have my lunch, and begin reading until I started writing my own journal about my feelings. Writing became therapeutic to me because it allowed me to feel lighter after every expression. I was opening doors on the inside of my soul that had been hindering in the dark gates of hell for so long. It was no wonder I always had dark people around me, influencing my dark path!

I was just about to start my meditation for the morning when Dr. Bakshi arrived knocking at my cell.

"Hello, Miss. Brown! Can I come in? I have some things I would like to speak to you about."

"Sure! You know you're always welcome, Doc!" I said with a chuckle.

She made her way into my cell and I could see the British officer whose real name was Pete. He's the worst breed of asshole to have to interact with within these prison walls. He had to know everything so he could find a way to violate your rights as a prisoner. He had many women doing sexual favours for him just because he knew who had the drugs and who was musclin' who. This was his form of bribery to keep him from informing the Warden about the drug game going on right under her nose. He used their families as weakness, or resorted to threatening them to believe they would be institutionally charged for longer periods of time. Most women cracked, but I would not…no matter what drugs he offered me. He was pig and I could smell him from a mile away. In the end he would be cooked for dinner—I just had to figure out a way to bring him down.

I completely ignored Officer Pete and put all my attention towards Dr. Bakshi.

"Give me a moment with the inmate," she said in a calm but stern voice.

Officer Pete winked at me but not before grabbing his crotch and slowly walking away with a smirk. He did this all behind Dr. Bakshi's back. When she noticed my eyes were looking beyond her, she turned around to look but Officer Pete had stopped. He began closing my cell door and Dr. Bakshi kept her eyes on him until he left.

"Now that we are alone I have some good news and bad news. Which one do you want first?"

I looked deeply into Dr. Bakshi's eyes to look for betrayal or a fucked up vibe, but I could not find anything.

"The bad," I said in a disappointing tone.

"OK. It's not anything we can't fix or workaround. I had to write a medical assessment for the Warden and she decided from the medical assessment that you would have to take these pills. She said with your actions, she felt it must be done and I can't go over the Warden's head. I convinced her that it was in your best interest if I gave you the medication myself because she wanted the officers to do it. I'm going to act like I am but the truth is, I'm not. In saying this, you will have to show symptoms like you have taken these pills. Symptoms such as drowsiness, fatigue, and obedient behaviour because that is the only way they will think you're taking them."

Dr. Bakshi was a down ass chick. I mean seriously, she could lose her job for this shit.

"OK!" I smiled.

"I'm doing this because I see something in you. You are not like a lot the people that come in here. You are different. You are also a baby, and I would not want that being done to my child, so I am not going to do it to you. I believe in you and I realize no one has showed you how to believe in yourself. Listen to your soul and find your path. I also realize sometimes we have to go through the darkness to find our light. I think you were brought to me as a gift and I am going to honour that. You have the spirit of a warrior and the light that shines around you, people are attracted to but you have to believe in it for it to shine bright. All is supposed to happen when it's meant. There is no such thing as luck or coincidence but there is destiny and free will. You chose this journey, so I know you will make it through the way you are supposed to. These prisons were built for us to continue as slaves. It is cheaper for them to house prisoners than it is to have them on the outside. It's a billion dollar business, just like war is."

"Like Tupac said: *money for wars, but can't feed the poor!*"

"Exactly and you must be aware of that on your path. Realize there are traps that have been put in place by a dark, corrupted force that is trying to kill us all but we have the key to freedom, it's inside us. Now, would you like the good news?"

"Yes, and thank you for all of this. I really do believe it!"

"Don't worry, I am doing this because I am supposed to. The good news is, you will be rewarded in a great way from me but I have some conditions. You must educate, train, and meditate daily. You must also stay away from drugs. That also means selling them. You have a responsibility on this earth to change the lives of others, and you have a gift sitting inside you waiting to be released."

"A gift? What gift?" I said, starting to laugh.

"This is not a joke! It's serious. The gifts you have are: one, the love you carry in your heart. It is a very sacred love and anyone you touch with it you will change their life in some way. Two, your writing is another gift to change the world. Your poems are like music to the ear and warmth to the soul. You must share them to help others. The last one you don't know about it, and once you realize the first two you will find it and get rid of the noise in your mind."

"OK? How do you know all this?"

"I don't question why or how. I accept and surrender to the purpose."

"OK." I said with skepticism.

"Remember my words! I am going to…"

"Wait! What's the reward?" I said grabbing Dr. Bakshi's hand.

"You will know once you receive it! Take care, and I will see you soon."

CHAPTER SIX: Voices

The ear of the leader must ring the voices of the people!
~Woodrow Wilson

"Help me! Help me! Help me!" the voice screamed in the distance.

I lay in my jail cell, half-awake from my sleep, to hear a voice echoing through my wall. I sat in silence listening to her voice asking for help repeatedly. It was coming from somewhere in the Maximum unit but I was still not sure if I was hearing things. I continued to listen in silence when I heard the screaming stop. It was then I knew they had brought another female into maximum. It was then I heard she was being beaten because immediately after the pause of silence came screams of agony. I wanted to cover my ears but I listened in horror. I also listened to remember what they did to me. Dr. Bakshi was right, I needed to be ready for war with these muthafuckas, but the only way I could do that was to be trained and strategize to take them down.

Her screams gave me the motivation to push further. Her torture blew life into my lungs. I got out of my bed and began working out. I started with push-ups, and for each scream I went down and waited for the next one until I rose up. I did not stop this until I could not hear her anymore. Her voice riddled my soul and angered my spirit to fight a war I never knew existed before. I trained for an hour in my cell, and once I was complete, I began my yoga and meditation. During this time my food was thrown into my cell and I was happy it was oatmeal. I had become use to the treatment of the officers, so I ignored them at this point. When I was ready to strike I would...and they would not expect it.

I had been getting more rigid with my diet and now I was vegan completely, so the officers had to feed me according to my diet. I never felt more alive. The officers loved my behaviour because I was not acting out, as Dr. Bakshi had instructed me to do. She visited my cell every day to act like she was giving me my medication. During that time, we talked and she continued to educate me on life, balance, moderation, love, and change. She made it clear for me to have any impact on the world I would have to change myself. I would have to find the true being that existed behind all the layers of pain and suffering that I had been exposed to. She also talked about forgiveness and let me know to have peace; I needed to forgive what had been done to me, while also forgiving what I had done myself. She said I carried anger that was deep rooted inside of me, with pain and fear. It was clear that until I did the inner work to heal, I would be stuck in the same places. She was right.

I knew that no matter how I tried to deny what she was saying, because of Shine trying to convince me of the more comfortable path I had taken all these years, I could not. She made me realize that my mind has to be separated from my ego Shine which was driving the wheel most of the time. Emily was my inner child who was in constant fear of Shine, or at times would have the strength to protect me from her.

The meditation and the yoga quieted Shine's loud, arrogant, and ignorant chatters of fear. She clung to whatever moments I was weak, or to the hurt emotions that would surface, but the more and more I fed her good solid love, the more she dissolved. No one ever taught me that I had to love myself to love the world. Dr. Bakshi helped give me that light again.

It felt like I was reaching lunch time in my cell and I knew that was the time Dr. Bakshi was coming. I checked my radio clock and I was right, it was 12pm. I just received the radio I had ordered from Canadian Tire from the time I was in medium. The officers kept it until I was obedient enough for them to give it to me. I was quite happy, as I could listen to music and find out what was happening in the world while also keeping track of clock time. I began cleaning up my cell when Dr. Bakshi arrived for my daily dose of pills.

"Can I come in?" she asked.

"Yes, I'm decent." I responded.

Dr. Bakshi entered my cell with a big smile that lit up the room as always. She was not wearing her normal white Doctor jacket that she typically wore.

"You look different today?"

"Yes, no jacket! I'm going to need you to get yourself dressed. I'm bringing you to the medical unit in the main building. I think it's time to check on some things with your physical health."

"Is something wrong?" I said, slightly worried.

"No, actually you're great! I just want to make sure you are good, so I'm going to do a physical. Plus, would you not like to get fresh air?"

"Fresh air?" I laughed.

"You know what I mean, Diamond. You're out of twenty-three-hour lock up!" she laughed back at me, shining her glistening teeth.

Her smile was so beautiful that it could get anyone caught up like I was now.

"Diamond!" she snapped.

"Yes!" I replied, breaking my daydream.

"Get ready! I will stand outside while you do so. Officer Melissa has insisted she bring you to the appointment with me, and so has the Warden!"

Just as I was about to respond, Officer Melissa came waddling in my cell.

"She's getting ready, we can wait outside," Dr. Bakshi insisted when addressing Melissa.

"Well what's with all the chitter chatter, let's get it moving Brown. I don't have all day!"

I did not even bother to make eye contact with her. I just started to look for my belongings to put on as they exited to stand outside my cell. I quickly got dressed. I could not wait to get outside.

"UP AGAINST THE WALL, BROWN!"

Officer Melissa did not even give me breathing room. I could still smell her morning breath like she had not eaten lunch yet. It was a rude, nasty smell, like someone just took a shit. I held my breath while I was being cuffed.

They decided to cuff my hands and feet because I was a high-risk threat, and especially since I had been dangerously offended. They were not going to take any risks with my history of behaviour. I remained silent and continued to follow their lead as I was escorted out of max. I could not wait to get a taste of what was going on in the medium, it seemed like forever. As I was walking through the Max unit, I was able to put a face to the voice of the other girl in max. She was being escorted to her cell with Officer Pete when she took notice of us. She immediately started chanting for help.

"Help me! Help me! Help…" it was short winded because Officer Pete carried her along through the Max units. She was Native, and looked like she had some serious mental issues. She had makeup drawn all over her face like she was a child trying to put on her parent's makeup. Her eyes were dark and lifeless with black mascara smudged all around them. She kept mumbling under her breath. She had dark red lipstick coloured on the side of her cheeks. Officer Pete continued to push her along to her cell. Her long dark black hair had not been combed and she looked like she had been violated. I got the impression quickly that Officer Pete was taking advantage.

I don't know why but I did. He did not pay any attention to us leaving. He kept his focus remained on her.

Dr. Bakshi watched them pass along. and it was like she felt what I felt and spoke.

"Is that inmate OK, Officer Pete?" she firmly asked.

"She's fine! She needs rest! She's been up all night freaking out in her cell. I just brought her outside to calm her down," he said.

He looked at me, and gave me the coldest look I had ever witnessed in this prison. I had not witnessed eyes like that since I had been on the streets. I looked at the girl and knew he was lying through his teeth. He knew I heard her screaming from last night while she was being tortured, why he gave me that look. He wanted to make sure I kept my mouth closed by intimidation and it worked. His evil eyes pierced into mine but I gave him back a shield of love and he quickly turned away.

"We're good here," he muttered, and kept moving.

I realized I would have to help her later or he would kill any kind of life she had left in her.

I was quickly escorted out of the Max unit and into the yard of the medium houses. I could not believe how much I longed to be there. My time there was smooth sailing, but it came with a price. For every dark experience there is a message of beauty waiting to be shared, if you pay attention enough to notice it. It will always lead you back to the true essence of who you really are.

"DIAMOND! I love you!" someone screamed from a distance.

I looked towards house five and I saw Blonde, Erica, and Fatback running across the field.

"Hiiiii!" Erica yelled until she got closer to me.

I smiled, but did not speak.

"Are you OK? I miss you!" Erica said.

I smiled, and as I was about to open my mouth to respond, that's when Officer Melissa spoke.

"GET AWAY FROM THE INMATE, OR ALL OF YOU WILL BE CHARGED!"

"Fuck off, Melissa! Charged for talking? It's a free country! Afraid she's going to bust your face again?" Erica said while chuckling.

"I'm fuckin' warning you Erica! BACK THE FUCK UP!"

"Or what? Or fuckin' what?"

Erica was right in Melissa's face and her white skin went to red real quick. Blonde grabbed Erica quickly and pulled her back before it escalated.

"Let's go!" Blonde said.

Her eyes locked with mine, and we both knew that Erica escalating shit would only make it harder for me with my time. It was like she felt my vibe and pulled Erica back.

"Did you get my letters Diamond? I write you every day! Why aren't you writing back? I love you!"

"We all love you!" Fatback said and they stepped back as I was escorted in the building.

"What letters is she talking about, and why have I not gotten any of my mail?"

Melissa paused for a long minute before responding.

"Your mail is under investigation?" she muttered.

"FOR FUCKIN' WHAT?"

Dr. Bakshi abrasively grabbed my arm to tame me. Her soft, petite brown hands were powerful. I quickly got a force of calmness over my body—they were trying to fuck with me because this was personal. This again was about Erica and the Warden Lauren, but of course she had to involve me. She involved me because I was Erica's weakness. I could get her to freak out in this prison and Lauren would get to control her. I'm sure Blonde was telling her the exact same thing right now.

I could feel Melissa watching me, waiting for a reaction but I put my head down and continued walking.

We arrived at the medical unit where Dr. Bakshi's office was, and we both waited for Melissa to remove the handcuffs she had put on me. I observed all the women as we walked through the main building, watching and talking as I made my way to the medical unit. It was interesting because I've never noticed any attention before. It was like the whole building stopped.

"Diamond, let's go get you checked out," Dr. Bakshi instructed.

We began making our way into the medial unit when Melissa tried to follow.

"Officer Melissa, you can wait outside while I check inmate Brown in my office thank you."

"Well don't take all day! I have my rounds to do in the other units."

"I understand that, and we won't be long," Dr. Bakshi said dismissing Melissa.

CHAPTER SEVEN: Lights Out

Every man must decide whether he will walk in the light
of the creative altruism or in the darkness
of destructive selfishness.
~Martin Luther King Jr.

It did not take long for Dr. Bakshi to give me a physical, but that was not the real reason for her wanting to bring me to her office. Dr. Bakshi felt they had private cameras in my cell and she wanted to warn me about the investigation the Warden was doing on me that I was not aware of. I thought that after they classified me to maximum security, I would just spend my time there. She let me know that the police had recently come to the prison requesting information about me. They wanted to go through my calls and letters. They thought I had something to do with X-Rated and Jeru's murder.

"Did you, Diamond?"

I took a long pause before I answered her but I had nothing to hide.

"No. They died when I was in here, and I had nothing to do with it."

"Why have you not called their families or reached out if these were your close childhood friends?" Dr. Bakshi inquired.

"How do you know they were my close childhood friends?" I asked with a puzzled look on my face.

"I have my ways! Now answer my questions because we don't have long, and I can only help you if let me but you have to be honest with me."

I could tell by the look Dr. Bakshi gave me along with the tone in her voice, that she was in no mood to play games or pry information out of me.

"I was weak and I could not handle it. Everyone deals with death differently. Some mourn, some celebrate, some people's lives never move on and some just begin life after the death of a loved one. I was not sure which path was mine and I still don't know. I have chosen to push those emotions aside in order to do my time," I said looking down.

I could not bring myself to look at her.

"That is not healthy, and I am sorry for your loss. I understand that the loss of your close friends must be hard to deal with."

"Ye. So, is that it?"

"I want to make sure you are OK."

"OK with what? I'm fine," I said brushing off any feelings that were trying to surface in my body.

The wounds for Jeru and X-rated were very deep. She was trying to search for something, but I had nothing to give.

"Healing is essential to moving forward. You have to feel the emotions. Sometimes even sit in them for a while, and feel the uncomfortableness so you can let it go. To run, avoid, or even try to hide those feelings will cause you problems later on when they decide to explode. It's unbearable to hide something that has wounded you so deeply. Please don't ignore me."

Dr. Bakshi grabbed my hand gently. She could feel my tense energy in the room.

"Thank you. Are we done now?" I said quietly.

I could not face her. I looked down on the ground as my tears were fighting to be held back. I was quickly interrupted with a big bang on the door.

"LET'S GET IT MOVING!" Melissa thumped on the door.

I jumped up along with Dr. Bakshi. She flung my hand and marched towards the door to open it.

"I am finishing the inmate's physical. You will not be disrespectful at this time, Melissa. You will wait until we are finished here."

Melissa's face went red again but something in Dr. Bakshi's tone and eyes put fear in her.

"I have rounds to do, is all, so I was just letting you know!"

"I am almost finished checking the inmate; we will be out shortly."

Dr. Bakshi finished my check up and slipped something into my pocket.

"You will need this, and you will know when you need it. Keep it safe, and keep it close to you!"

"What..."

"Don't ask questions, just get going before they suspect something," Dr. Bakshi ordered.

I was escorted quickly out of the medical unit to find a line of inmates waiting to see Dr. Bakshi. Melissa shackled me impatiently, and I was on my way back to max. All the women kept watching me and talking, but it was all out of respect. I could see it in their eyes. They honoured me.

"D.B.D BROWN!" someone shouted, from the line of women waiting.
I did not bother to respond. I continued walking, ignoring them. The cheers of admiration made it completely harder for me to face what I had to go back to. I continued through the compound when I heard Erica shout out: "I LOVE YOU DIAMOND! PLEASE WRITE ME!"

Melissa pushed me along through the compound to the Max unit. My arrival was bitter all around; I had to meditate to put my emotions to rest. My ego was convincing my mind of all these negative things that I should be doing, and I was thinking way too much. I needed silence. The silence that would once drive me mad was becoming a soothing nest for peace and tranquility.

I settled in my unit and started setting up for meditation when I remembered Dr. Bakshi's gift. I removed it from the pocket of my jogging suit—it was a miniature sharp knife that was in a sealed leather black case. I could not believe my eyes. The knife could cut through anyone's heart instantly because of the sharpness of the blade. I pulled out the knife and a little white slip of paper fell on the concrete cell floor. I grabbed it quickly and put both back in my pocket. I looked around my cell to see if there were cameras but I could not see anything. I hid the knife and letter then proceeded to tear my whole cell apart in search of these cameras.

It was not long before I found a voice recorder glued to the inside of my toilet bowl. I did not make a sound. All breaths that I had in me waiting to exhale, I held them. As silently and softly as I could, I removed the tiny black and silver voice recorder. It was very small and also undetectable. I quickly found the mute button and put it back right where it came from. Anything that happened in my cell they would not hear—period—but I had another purpose for this voice recorder. I would figure out a way to keep this charade up but also use it to my advantage. I would turn it on mute and off mute when needed to. I would not make them any wiser that I had found this. This was a violation of my rights, but I did not give a fuck. These muthafuckas were playing the wrong bitch.

I grabbed the letter and opened it. It was from Dr. Bakshi so I knew I had to discard it quick. It would only be a matter of time before the guards came to do rounds.

Diamond,

This sacred knife has been blessed for you. The knife is for your protection and survival. It has many gifts if you use it only for protection. It will also direct you to answers you never knew existed. Please talk to the knife and name it. Love it like a child and it will love you back in

all ways. Do not let anyone discover it or touch it, as that will remove all protection for you.
Green Tara

I was not sure what to think of this, so I followed the instructions without question. I organized my cell back before the guards came to do their rounds and hand out our evening meals. I began my routine meditation to feel centred and at peace. I needed it more and more—my whole body craved it. I was beginning to open my third eye to a world I never knew existed: an unseen world of universes and light life forms of energy. It was captivating yet calming. I could see them directing me in my inner travels, to a place unknown to man. A place that you had to unlock the keys of your soul to find. The physical world could not unlock these doors. Man in the physical could not unlock these doors nor could science. The answers were inside you where your limitless soul existed. A place foreign to many but understood by some: the watchers, the masters, the gatekeeper and the one of all infinite. They keep calling, but I had not yet figured out who they were. I was still attached to the physical world, therefore freedom was not mine to grasp…just yet.

"COUNT!"

I was interrupted by my meal being thrown in my cell. My peaceful travels had thrown me back into my body, to face the bullshit physical world I was currently trapped in.

"STAND UP! You know the routine!" Officer Pete shouted out to me.

I did as I was told and waited for them to confirm my body count before they closed my cell block door. I did not entertain his charade of a game; it was enticing, even though I avoided it, but I knew it was a trap.

The night arrived quickly and I was gaining all the information I could. I hardly noticed the clock as I was so busy on this quest for enlightenment. I felt with each moment I had so much more information, knowledge, and understanding to retain. I was eating the fruits of knowledge like it was an everlasting supply. I could not get enough. The more I learned, the more I strategized for a battle I could not see, smell, taste or touch…but it was coming.

CHAPTER EIGHT: Violations

**To deny people their rights is to challenge
their very humanity.
~Nelson Mandela**

*So you think now that you met Dr. Bakshi that I still
don't control you? Bitch you must be crazy. I will forever
run a bitch like you! You ain't nothing but a punk! You will
never do anything with your life. You need to figure out a
way to get drugs in this max shit before I...*
"The voice of doubt or fear. As everything that is
not love is fear," As Dr. Bakshi would say. I could see her
gentle perfect smile glistening in the dream state I was in,
with the cold sweats dripping off my forehead, rolling
down to my lips. The salty flavour reminded me I was still
alive and locked down in this institution. Shine would test
my faith. She would be the first fight I had to conquer
before I could strategize for war with anyone else. The less
Shine surfaced, the stronger I became as I continued on my
mission, digging deeper for answers.
The cold sweats mixed with Shine's threats had
awoken me from my sleep. I went to the toilet and flushed
it while I grabbed my sacred knife, but not before
remembering to put the voice recorder on mute. I held the
knife praying for protection from Shine and the prison
guards, until I was at peace and could no longer feel the
lower energies. This was the best time for me to do a
journal entry to express my feelings and gain some clear
perspective.

*Hello,
It has been a while since we last connected and I
wanted to express the paranoia in my dreams because of
Shine. She is trying hard to conquer, but I'm dominating*

her. With each moment that passes I feel more alive now more than ever. As I sit here on my bunk thinking of yesterday's rut, I realize it can be done and it will be done. I will achieve greatness for the battle is mine, and mine alone! I can do…"

"HELLLLLLPPP MEEEEEE!" the voice echoed in the distance.

Then it went silent again. I stopped writing instantly and sat in the darkness of my cell listening when a young, Aboriginal, beautiful woman appeared before me in my cell. She was dressed like a warrior princess, like she had just come from a Pow Wow. I looked closer and it was the girl I saw in the hallway. Only this time she looked stunning. There was not a strand of hair out of place, and her makeup was done to perfection.

How the fuck did she get in my cell? I thought to myself as I jumped back so far, almost falling off my bunk backwards. Then I heard Dr. Bakshi's voice whispering: *Do not fear for fear is an illusion created by you. Laugh in the uncomfortableness!*

She was gone when I was ready to face her, but her energy lingered in the distance. I ended up slapping myself to divert thoughts of myself going crazy, but I stung my face so hard I could not help but laugh. I was awake and I knew who I saw…or so I thought I did.

I turned the recorder off mute and went back to my bed to sleep before the guards did their two a.m. rounds. I kept the knife with me for protection because I did fear everything that was happening. The unseen puts fear in us. We cannot explain it, but what if we are not supposed to explain it? What if we are to just accept things as they are? The "what if" question can lead you in a maze! The dark silence was clutching my body, sensually. I had questions but no answers. I had to accept things as they were.

The next day was a quiet as I started my morning routines of working out and meditating. I tried to get the experiences off my mind, but every time I started to think I saw her face asking me for help. I had to figure out a way to get to her or speak to her. I prayed for the answer to come to me, but silence was all that remained. I closed my eyes, trying to heighten my senses to hear the voices, but all I could hear were muffled whispers in the distance. I continued concentrating and focusing on my pineal gland when she appeared.

"HELP ME! HELP ME! HELP MEEEE PLEASE!"

The voices got louder when I realized she was chanting from her prison cell. I opened my eyes and listened, clutching my sacred knife. I moved closer and put my ear against the concrete wall, and her voice got louder. How was this possible when this was concrete?

"BROWN!"

I jumped out of my trance of thought.

"ENTERING THE UNIT! STAND BACK!"

I quickly jumped off my bed, hid my knife in my underwear, and clicked the off mute button on the voice recorder. I was just in time as the prison guards were entering my cell.

"WHAT'S GOING ON BROWN?" Officer Pete said as he pushed himself into my cell. He did not have any prison guards with him and that made me worry. "What's going on? I know you hear me."

I was frozen for words but that did not seem to matter to this pig Pete. He entered my cell without an invitation and I knew he was up to no good. I could smell his foulness from a mile away and the smirk on his face confirmed that he was up to no good.

"So how you like it here?" he said, making his way closer and closer to me.

"I'm fine."

"That's all? Just fine?" he said, standing in front of my bunk.

I moved back, pushing my back against the concrete wall. He slid closer, now touching my leg. I immediately jumped up and moved.

"WHAT do you want?" I demanded.

The energy in my cell was full of tension and I could feel the fear waiting to explode in the distance. He followed me to the corner of my cell, still smiling and inching closer and closer. He was trying to figure out a way to advance himself on me, but I kept moving around.

"Don't make this difficult, Brown!"

"What do you want?" I repeated.

"You know the answer to that."

I moved towards my cell door and his smile grew wider because I got backed into a corner.

"You're gonna make a good inmate during your time here aren't you?"

He was right in my face reaching to grab on to me. I could smell the left over beer sitting on his breath; his eyes were dark and cold as he leaned in, getting closer to me. He jumped back quickly when there was a bang on my cell door.

"Are you decent, Brown?"

"Yes! Come in," I said with a sigh of relief.

Officer Pete moved away from me, no longer smiling of course. He gave me that same evil look that he gave me when I passed him and the young lady that visited me the other night. This just confirmed my feelings about him.

"Hello?"

It was Dr. Bakshi and Melissa. I was saved for only a moment though because who knew when this vulture would be back to try and violate again. Dr. Bakshi entered my cell and quickly understood while continuing to assess what was happening.

"Are you OK, Brown?" she asked, but her full undivided attention was on Officer Pete.

"I'm OK," I said in an unconfident whisper.

Melissa had come in the cell behind her and they both were assessing Officer Pete.

"We need to go for our rounds, Pete."

Melissa quickly diffused the situation by removing Officer Pete from my cell. Dr. Bakshi watched him leave with a look of disgust.

"Are you OK?" she asked me, but I knew better than to tell the truth because of the voice recorder that was currently recording.

"I'm fine."

"What was going on in here?"

I grabbed my pad and pen to begin writing.

"Nothing," I said, as I started writing out what happened as well as letting her know there was a voice recorder recording our conversations. I also told her where it was located. Dr. Bakshi's face almost turned red with embarrassment. I sat so frustrated and upset but I knew I could not take this battle on alone. I let her know I needed her help and so did the other girl being tortured. I explained what I had been hearing, and she let me know it was not the first time. She agreed for us to come up with a plan to get us both out of the Max unit, but I would have to be patient while she worked her end.

Dr. Bakshi let me know she would work on a plan and come back to me in the next couple days. I let her know we did not have long with Officer Peter. He was a demon in disguise and whatever he wanted to do to us he would, because he realized we were vulnerable to him. Dr. Bakshi promised she would have a plan very soon but I would have to hang in there and fight him if he approached me. She also let me know that she had visited the other lady in max and would help the both of us out.

CHAPTER NINE: The Plan

Plan, plot, strategize, and bomb first.
~Tupac Shakur

I was surprised when I received my mail, and of course Officer Pete had to be the one delivering. I had been in my cell working on poetry and mastering the art of stillness when he arrived. He had a stack of mail and I was excited to get to reading the letters and responding. Officer Pete threw the mail in my cell without a word—he did not bother to enter or engage in any conversation. His skin was rosy and starting to look tough like leather. You could tell whatever he was battling in his own life, it was getting the best of him. This was none of my concern but yet the heart I had would always see the struggle in another human being and wish I could help them. He closed back my cell and I ran to start opening my letters. The first letter I opened was from Renee.

Dear Diamond,
How are you? I have been writing for a while now with not one word. Are you OK? I know you must be hurting at the loss of your friends, but your family is still here for you and we want to help in any way we can.
Things out here are not the same. It's like everyone has pressed on with life but I am missing my best friend. Some days it's easier than others because of your niece who is getting bigger by the minute. Her Father, now…that's a whole different story. I mean, someday I want to ring his neck, and the other days we have so much in common it's like we are best friends. It's a twisted relationship but as I grow with our daughter, I've started to realize that her birth has hindered his growth. He is so much in a daze with

life and in a cloud of smoke that I can barely talk to him without chewing his fucking head off.

Anyway enough about my shit. How are you? Are you OK? How are you eating in there, and why the silence? I just want to know you are OK.

Love always,
Renee
P.S. If I don't hear from you soon I'm going to come there and raise up hell in that place!

Her words hit my chest like a knife piercing through my heart. The familiar words hit home for me and I wanted to cry but I held back. I held back the pain of being away from my family. I had to make that pain my ammunition out of this place. If they knew my family was my weakness, they would break me. Lauren would use it against me. I continued on to the next letter and it was from Jiffs.

Shine,
What's good, man? It's been too long and the whole block misses you. Things done changed with you and Jeru gone. I mean shit has died down but dem boys still lurkin' thinkin' we had somethin' to do with Jeru's death. I keep asking Renee for you, man. Hit a nigga back and know I held you down. Holla at me, man.
One

I had to write Renee back and she would have to figure out the code by speaking to Jiffs, because if I wrote normally they would not ship the letter. I used the blood code because I knew Jiffs could decode it. He was not a blood, but he was a smart nigga so he knew how to decode something so simple yet undetectable by some. It's interesting…after years of oppression, black folks found a way to get around any and everything no matter what the

---

situation. There was something hidden deep within us that always allows us to conquer anything we face. The strength just surfaced from within. A divine plan was in the works and I could not wait to get out so I could get my plans in motion. I began sitting in silence with the pen and pad in my hand. I wanted to let Renee know I was in danger in the max unit. My rights as a prisoner had been violated and I was being forced medication that I did not need—also, I was classified as a dangerous offender. I had to express this in a way to get the word out but I did not want Renee to react because that would not help. I crafted a four page letter and revealed everything they had done to me. I expressed that I needed her to go to the media and look about starting a blog. I wanted to use the blog as a way to express my poetry and expose the conditions I was living in, in the prison. I wanted to connect with the public so I could use my voice to speak for all the prisoners. I was going to fight these muthafuckas some way and if it was not in here it was going to be on road. They would not get away with it.

I continued crafting my letter in code to Renee and it felt like a ton of bricks had been released from inside of me. I could not help but cry. It had been a long time coming. I cried for every moment of bullshit I had been through on this earth. I cried asking God, *why me*? Why did I have to go through this? I was about to wallow in my self-pity, but that was just a plan of destruction.

It did not take long for the guards to begin harassing me in my cell after my letters had arrived. I guess I was too quiet for their comfort, because they decided to strip search my cell.

I was moved from my cell as they came rushing inside; I had to stand outside and watch them strip apart my cell. Luckily, I kept my knife in my underwear waiting for Officer Pete to try me. They flipped my cell upside down going through every book, letter, and all my personal hygiene products. They threw everything on the centre of my cell floor, but I did not get a rise or a reaction. Period. I observed Officer Pete, Melissa, and Mike, all basking in their glory trying to get a reaction out of me…but I remained silent. I knew they had no information on me that warranted them doing this: they just did it for power trippin' control. By the time they were finished, my cell was a complete disaster, and the officers brought me back inside to clean up the mess. I remained silent and continued to breathe.

My dinner was thrown into my cell about ten minutes after I began cleaning; I checked the toilet to see if the voice recorder was still around, but it was gone. I figured they probably wanted to listen to it so that they could report back to the Warden about my letters. That must have been the reason for the search. I anticipated their return sooner than later because I knew they had every intention of putting that voice recorder back where they got it.

It wasn't long after Dr. Bakshi came to give me my daily dose of medication. I hope she had some good news about her plan of action because I was ready to get this ball on the road.

"How are you today, Diamond?" she said. Her energy was a bit off, but I continued with our normal fake routine of her administering my medications.

"I'm good, and you?" I said, sitting on my bunk beside Dr. Bakshi.

She was dressed in a white blouse and dark blue jeans. She had on a pair of low heeled black boots, her hair was pulled up in a messy bun, she had no makeup on, and was natural. Her beauty radiated throughout my cell.

"I'm ok! They ruined your cell. Is all well?"

I knew she meant the sacred knife she had given me.

"All is good! I just have to clean up this shit. Any good news yet about my visitation?" I actually meant our plan of action…and Dr. Bakshi knew exactly what I meant.

"All is going as it should. The application has been submitted and now we wait for approval from the Warden. I will let you know as soon as the time is right."

"OK!" I said with a feeling of hope.

"You should get approved sooner than later, because I submitted it myself."

Dr. Bakshi quickly grabbed a pen and paper off the floor to write.

I will be visiting your cell tonight when the guards go to do rounds in the compound. I have to get you both out of here. I am going to give you tools to help you get to Carrie and a map of passage to escape this prison. I have a bad feeling about what is going on in this prison. This is beyond you. This has more to do with the messed up officers working here alongside the Warden. They do not value themselves therefore they cannot and will not value your lives. There is a darkness they carry deep within them. You both are prey. You need to get out while you can. I am taking a big risk doing this, but I have no other option.

Escape? Was she crazy? How the fuck was I going to escape with this girl? I trusted Dr. Bakshi's words, but I was not sure I would be able to get this completed. These prison guards were like hawks waiting for prey. They missed nothing. She saw the concern on my face and continued writing.

I know this sounds far-fetched but it's either life or death. This is your choice to make.

This was much more serious than I ever thought. Dr. Bakshi knew much more than she was leading on. I did not say a word but my mind went on speed mode with all the questions I had that I could not ask. I just followed her lead and would wait patiently for direction. Dr. Bakshi ripped up the letter and flushed it. She gave me a long bear hug and exited my cell.

CHAPTER TEN: Nightmares

Who's to say dreams and nightmares aren't
as real as the here and now?
~John Lennon

"Emily! It's time to go now! We have to pack our things. We have been in Jamaica for a long time now. We must get back home and back to regular routine, darling."

"But I don't want to leave, Grandma! I don't want to leave!"

"We must, darling, and don't worry, we will come back very soon."

"OK, Grandma!"

I could still feel his leathery skin as he forcefully pushed himself inside me. His alcoholic breath breathing heavily over my body. I wanted to pull out my sacred knife and stab him repeatedly, but this was not the time.

"Oooh, baby you feel so good! Your dark wet pussy has been yearning for me," Officer Pete said as he forcefully held my hands and feet down while he pushed harder and harder inside me. He had ripped my clothes off in the middle of the night after he entered my cell as I was sleeping. I should have known better than to fall asleep, because I was no longer safe with this pig muthafucka around all the time. I saw the way he looked at me. Like I was a piece of meat he was hunting to eat.

I did not make a sound, but the tears rolled down my face repeatedly like small waterfalls. I was helpless, and he overpowered my strength to fight back. His breaths got hotter and heavier until he collapsed on my chest. I was in horrifying disgust. This nasty pig had violated every piece of dignity I had left within me. He let go of my hands and removed his heavy black boots from holding down my feet. He quickly stood up and did up his pants while his keys jingled in the distance. He had this smirk on his face that I would never forget, and his blue eyes turned dark. My vision and sound started to become blurry as If I was in a dream that I could not wake up from. I laid there on the concrete floor crying without a word or noise.

"Get yourself together. Morning rounds will be starting soon. This is our little secret. I don't want this to get out to anyone or I will have no choice but to take matters into my own hands."

I was at a loss for words. The disgust, pain, and fear that rose up inside of me was dreadful. I started to feel like I was suffocating. My breaths became shorter and my chest began to tighten. My mind was racing all over the place replaying the violations that took place against my mind, body, and soul. I could not move and I did not want to move. I was in agony from the inside out. I sat there trembling in the dark. Officer Pete left my cell and I continued to sit in silence, rocking back and forth waiting for his return.

The morning did not take long to arrive and I could not close my eyes for the life of me. Every noise I heard in the distance startled my spirit. I got up finally after the burning sensation started to throb—my legs and buttocks from sitting and lying on the concrete floor for so long. I made my way to my sacred knife and was relieved it was still there. I held it close to my heart and prayed for protection. I put it away and began to get myself ready for a shower. I knew Melissa would be making her rounds to bring me to bathe.

I had never longed for a prison shower so much in my life. I sat there in my towel waiting with my thoughts racing. *How? What? When?* The questions kept coming up in my mind of how I was going to kill this muthafucka and escape out of this prison. Dr. Bakshi was right when she said I was in danger. Either way I played this, I could not stay in this prison. I would have to deal with constant violations from Officer Pete because if I reacted, I would have to deal with being treated like an animal caged up to suffer the worst types of conditions. This was the worst fuckin' nightmare and the fucked up part was, I was not dreaming.

"SHOWER!"

I jumped off my bed and made my way to my cell door to be handcuffed and taken to the showers. Melissa, as fat as she was, did not miss a beat when it came to her work routine. No matter how she waddled down the hallways.

I was escorted to the showers and could not wait to have my skin scrubbed. I felt like I still had his smell on my body. I turned on the hottest possible temperature of water, let it run down on me and soothe my skin. I wanted to burn the smell of him off my body. His nasty bodily fluid had been released inside of me and I was trying to scrub as hard as I could all over my body to get the thoughts out of my head. When I realized I was being watched. It was her. She entered in the shower beside me and she did not have on make-up. She was beautiful. I looked away quickly, but she made her way closer to where I stood standing bare naked feeling disgusted with myself. She smiled at me showing her clean, white teeth, and then started to speak.

"PIGS!" she yelled while making loud snorting noises in the shower. I could not help but laugh, as disturbed as I was about what just happened.

"PIGSSS DIRTY PIGSSSS!" she yelled. She stripped off her clothes and danced in the shower. Playing in the water like a child in the tub. She was splashing the water all over the place and laughing to herself like it was nobody's business. The shower area in the max was an open concept. It was not closed off at all. Everyone could see everyone showering to degrade the women even more. Either that, or it was not completed yet, and our rights were being violated. The white tiles glistened and the floors were spotless; we were the first to be using the area upon our arrival.

I would never be showing my body naked and it was so funny to see this young, goddess of beauty so free. Her energy radiated around me and I could not do anything but enjoy the moment. She began splashing me with the water, and I splashed her back, laughing.

"CUT THE FUCKIN' BULLSHIT OUT!" Melissa interrupted.

We both got startled out of our moment of bliss as we stood staring at Melissa. She had clearly been standing there long enough to see the two of us playing, naked. I grabbed my blue bathing towel and covered up my body.

"JONES! Continue on with your shower."

"Ocikomsis nakatew," she said loud enough for the both of us to hear.

I had no clue the words she spoke, but it did not sound nice. Her face had changed to the anger of a lion hunting prey. She began breathing loud like a dog panting. She stood for a moment looking at Melissa who was waiting for a reason to react, but Jones turned around, continuing her shower in peace. I removed my towel again and quickly finished my shower, noticing Melissa standing her ground firmly watching the two of us in order.

Jones kept looking over at me like she was going to say something, but she was humming a song I did not know as she finished her shower. The music resonated with me like I knew the song but could not place my finger on it. As I grabbed my towel and got myself ready to stand by Melissa and wait for Jones to finish, she spoke again.

"Pehtam," she said.

I smiled as if I knew the words she spoke when she spoke again.

"Iskwew," I smiled again politely.

"Understand your beauty, don't hide it. You have a gift we all want to see," she whispered loud enough for me to hear her words. As I began to look away and blush, an image flashed before me. It was the native Goddess I saw in my cell. When I looked at Jones she was completely different, her eyes dark, and her body limping along as we made our way back to our cell block unit. She did not look back at me…period. It was like she was not of this world or something. Maybe it was just my blurry vision because I had not slept enough the night before.

"LET'S KEEP IT MOVING!" Melissa barked as we both dragged ourselves back to our units.

When I entered my cell, I could still hear her voice whispering in my cell. She was repeating words in her language. Each word she said three times. I got light headed and sat down on my bunk. It must have been the hot shower and lack of sleep. I laid there in my towel in silence when my eyes started closing. This max unit was really starting to get to me. I needed to get out and very soon.

CHAPTER ELEVEN: Gifts

*Health is the greatest gift, contentment the greatest
wealth, faithfulness the best relationship.*
~Buddha

I was in the deepest, soothing sleep when Dr.
Bakshi arrived knocking at my cell door with Officer Pete.
When they unlocked my cell and I saw Officer Pete, I
almost fell off my bunk.

"Diamond, are you OK?" Dr. Bakshi asked rushing
over to my aid. I nodded without speaking a word in that
pig's presence.

"We are fine here Officer Pete, you can go now. I
will handle the inmate and if I need your assistance I will
let you know."

Officer Pete gave me the longest stare and I could
feel it. His energy was crippling my core with a shooting
pain straight down my spine—the wrath of his energy all
through my body. I did not look at him. I sat there in
silence keeping my eyes glued to the concrete floor.

He exited my cell and I took a breath of relief. I ran
to the toilet bowl to check if the voice recorder was there
and to my surprise it was. How and when it got back, I
didn't know. Maybe the shower trip with Melissa? It was
either Officer Pete or Jason who could have put the voice
recorder back, but I knew it had to be Officer Pete. My
intuition demanded that I listen to my gut feeling and not
deny the answer. I quickly motioned for Dr. Bakshi to
remain silent.

I grabbed a pen and paper for us to write down our
true expressions as we continued the charade of masking
our real feelings on the down low.

"How are you Diamond? I came to administer your
medication for the day."

"I'm good! A bit tired because I had a rough sleep last night."

"I can prescribe sleeping pills that won't affect your current medication if you're OK with that."

I began writing the truth of what occurred the previous night, and told her I need out as soon as possible. I quickly wrote:

He raped me last night! I need to get out of here now! Or he's going to continue and end up killing me or the Jones lady in the other cell unit.

Dr. Bakshi wrote back:

Who raped you?

Officer Pete. Please tell me you have a plan for us to get out of here.

She responded with a slight smirk on her face:

I do why and that's why I came to see you so early. I had a dream last night that something was wrong. I am going to come back Thursday morning to get you both out of here. I have put in an order to take you both for medical examines that I cannot facilitate here.

I was not impressed with her plan and had no idea what she smiling about.

Thursday morning is four days away! How am I supposed to bear it with this pig? Holy fuck!

I was livid! How did she expect me to just grin and bear this shit?

Please do your best. I promise I will get you both out of here. You will both make your escape from the hospital. I will give you money and a car to go into hiding. I have some good connections so I assure you, you won't be found.

"All better now. Get some rest. I will see you tomorrow morning. Maybe try to get some reading done; I know that helps me when I cannot fall asleep"

Dr. Bakshi grabbed the paper and flushed it down the toilet. I did not want her to leave but I knew that her plan was the best, and only option we had. The only thing about this plan that sat hard on my chest was that I could not contact my family, period. I would have to start a new life. So many thoughts began running through my mind. Why was God doing this to me?

Dr. Bakshi left my cell and my normal routine of getting my inner spirit at peace had gone out the window. I was left lost with a bag of emotions surfacing that I could not contain. My chest started tightening again and my breaths became shorter. I started getting crazy thoughts of stabbing myself over and over again. I could envision the blade of a knife going in and out of my chest slowly, as I smiled at the pain.

Just do it! End it! You're a waste of a life! I heard Shine repeating in the distance of my thoughts.

When I looked down on my bed, there was a crumpled up piece of paper. I thought it was the conversation Dr. Bakshi and I just had, so I opened it to make sure. To my surprise, it was something completely different.

I will get you out of here and your life will truly begin as the light you are. I have a special gift for you when you leave these walls. Something you could never imagine. Just be as patient as you can while playing the game of strategy. We strike when they least expect it. Free your mind in meditation and these conditions will not affect you. Freedom awaits. It's yours to have. The gift of life is a learning lesson that you must accept and surrender to. Believe there is a greater plan for all. This is just a phase you must endure, to prepare you for what's to come. You have so much more to live for.

I wanted to crawl up in a ball and cry. I knew the best thing for me was to meditate. Releasing the emotions in stillness. The constant chatter of my mind was enough to blow my brains out. I placed the towel on the concrete prison ground as I continued to remain naked. Sitting in my meditation position facing the sun when she appeared.

"Kisâkihitin." she said softly.

I sat there wondering if I was dreaming again. She was beautifully dressed in a different outfit this time but still looked like an exquisite Goddess from an Aboriginal tribe. She had a beautiful beaded blue and yellow headdress with a feather attached to the side. Her matching traditional dress was mesmerizing. Her matching feathered earrings lit up the beauty and glow of her natural skin. This time she had no makeup on. She began dancing around my cell and I was really starting to trip.

We are more alike than you know! Free spirits never die. No matter how we are hunted and attacked because of our gifts. The physical world is nothing to the spiritual world. It is only a test of experience and therefore we must celebrate. To new beginnings my dear!

Her words were loud but the room was silent.

She continued dancing as if she was at pow wow, smiling and twirling in her glory.

We chose these paths and there is one destiny for all. You have a purpose. Enjoy the experience and return back home with your knowledge to teach everyone. They are all waiting for you.

And just like that she was gone. I did not know what to think or feel so I just sat in the same position. Her words resonated deep within my soul and the message hit home for me. I began my meditation mantras aloud and each time I spoke it got louder. My soul was begging to be released from the prison my mind had fooled it to believe in. It was a trick and a trap which I had become victim to. I chanted louder and louder until my body froze and my spirit danced in front of me. A sacred, unexplainable dance that was so beautiful in existence but felt forbidden. My master had appeared before me dancing also. Guiding me to a place unknown to the eye, but known to the infinite soul. I went deeper into the cosmic ocean, entering dimensions and worlds I never knew existed. The calmness that surfaced within me cleared away any pain I was to face or had experienced. I did not think to question the process for my mind was still as my soul danced with the infinite, divine, sacred, geometry of the one.

CHAPTER TWELVE: Acceptance

Once we accept our limits, we go beyond them.
~Albert Einstein

The others had disappeared from my mind as my body and soul were forming as one from within. The physical reality was but a dream and I was the viewer of its movie. I caught myself laughing a lot in my prison cell. The travels to the cosmic bed of light and spirit increased, bringing about a piece of peace I could not explain. Experience is the only way to understand this wisdom. The mind is at a lower consciousness to understand and grasp this wisdom.

Officer Pete visited my cell every night, violating my body, but my mind and soul were free. I was protected each time he violated me, like I was outside of my body watching and observing his acts of darkness. All while gaining the wisdom needed to shed my light on this matter. I did not respond as he aggressively played out his hidden desires on my body. Entering every hole he could on my body that was accessible. Scratching, pulling, and pushing like I was a piece of cattle he had taken over. He started to get angrier at my limp, physical temple that remained non-responsive to his demons. He got more and more aggressive each night he entered my prison cell. As I watched him doing this, my spirit longed for prayer and forgiveness. He was a broken spirit. Lost and confused, like I was. I was no one to judge his actions even if it was they were against me.

The darkness of this world is not yours to gain, for the light will lead you on your path of destiny. I heard the words of her voice whisper softly in my ear, but what lingered were his venomous words of hate spewing out his mouth. I knew better though—these words were all out of hatred for himself.

"Look at you! You ugly fuckin' gorilla! You can't even fuck right. Look at you! You fuckin' mute! All you do is lay there!" he said as he finished, and began exiting my prison cell in a rage. I continued looking at him without any judgement or reaction. His emotions were surfacing all on his own. I did not have to do anything at all. He did everything at each moment to himself. My silence turned into a weapon he no longer could fight without facing himself in the mirror.

"You're just like that crazy bitch in the next cell. You must have the same mental disease because the two of you act exactly the same. Dumb bitches who can't do shit but lay there and stare," He exited my prison cell in a haste.

The days were moving by in slow motion, but I had no grasp of the time. Time was becoming non-existent the more I travelled into the unknown. My meditations were getting longer and longer, but more fulfilling each time. The warmth that calmed any uneasy feelings, became more present and removed any pain or suffering that tried to linger. I started to hear voices and see light forms that called me into worlds that were unknown to mankind in form. The formless world of spiritual liberty was becoming my home and my salvation of peace.

Dr. Bakshi returned each morning to falsely administer my medication and extract our plan of escape. On this particular morning when she arrived, I had no words of grief, but rather silence of peace and that was all that remained.

"You are humble. I feel the softness of your energy. You are finding your way to love and truth," she said with excitement.

Thursday was two days away and the medical external check-up she requested got approved. I was happy to finally be putting our plan into place. The good news came as a surprise to me because I was expecting her request to be denied. Regardless, Dr. Bakshi was lining her ducks up in a row.

"How is everything?" she asked politely, but not expecting an honest answer as we were still being recorded. I answered honestly anyway.

"I am present. That's all I really have today," I said. I did not have much left to talk about because it was time to take action. She also knew what time it was.

When Dr. Bakshi left, I continued to wait for the guards to do rounds before I began my routine. I did not want to be interrupted once I got into my travels, and I also wanted to get rest for the next couple days. The morning was at a peaceful bliss in harmony. It was a perfect setting for me to explore the other dimensions and talk to the others guiding this process of light. The process was like night changing into day. Something you cannot explain but you understand it needs to occur.

It was becoming just what is. There was no argument or resistance by my egoic mind. I accepted all that was and is, in the now. Each moment manifesting the energy and thoughts I was giving out to the universe. The higher my spiritual travels became, the more at peace I became with each moment. The more I could accept each moment that was to come.

My clairvoyant six senses were developing at a fast pace. It was like I was being pulled through this process for an unknown truth I had to teach the world, all stemming from a higher source. I was honoured to be the chosen light/life to teach this truth to the world. To be able to teach by experience was an honour within itself, while the textbook knowledge was to continue building up this society. A knowledge that was limited. The education I was learning was not taught in school and as I questioned everything critically, I realized some things just are. There is no need for questions unless you are ready to do the research in order to find the answers.

After I completed my routine, I realized I needed to get word to my family. I needed them to know that I would be escaping this prison and I would connect with them as soon as I was able to. In code, I began writing a letter to Renee.

> *Dear Renee,*
> *I hope this letter reaches you in time. The conditions of this prison have become very dangerous and I will no longer subject myself to these conditions. I am escaping to the outside. I will be in hiding for a while until I am able to surface and connect with y'all. Words cannot express the horrifying treatment I have received here in this prison. The correctional system is not for our people for we have been trapped to lose who we are as individuals. They have tried to take away all the good I have in me so they could in turn, turn me into the animal they see me as. They have violated any rights I have as a prisoner while emotionally, physically, and sexually abusing me. They have tried to drug me until my brain was no longer functional. I realized that continuing in this prison means death. A death that I would rather not face if I do not have to. My spirit has always been free and I will continue on my journey in life that way. The rules of this society created by a corrupt, greedy group of individuals will not hold me without will. I realize now that my purpose on this earth is to shed light by using my experiences to change and inspire others. I will always fight to find a way to be free of captivity.*
> *I hope that you and the family are OK. And no matter what you do, please keep this information between yourself and our FAMILY only!*
> *Love always,*
> *Diamond*

P.S. If anything happens to me and God forbid I do not return home, please share this letter with everyone and also share this letter to the people of our world so they too are aware. I want them to know no matter what the situation is, we can all overcome to help others. We must help others to see the light and believe in the power each of us possesses.

CHAPTER THIRTEEN: Escape

*They who dream by day are cognizant of many things
which escape those who dream only by night.*
~Edgar Allan Poe

The droplets of water touched my chocolate skin gently, grazing down my body. I watched the patterns in a misty daydream. The transparency of water was a gift within itself that I used to take for granted. A true healer. I had yet to understand deep down its existence. I was in the showers alone. I had not heard or witnessed Ms. Jones. She was silent, and that was an indication something was happening or going to happen. It was a vibe I got as I started to think about her while finishing my shower. I grabbed my grey towel and organized the hygiene products that I had brought from my cell with me.

Thursday had arrived much earlier than I expected, but I guess with the consistent meditation and workout routine I had created, it only made sense. Time was flying but time did not exist all at the same time. I quickly exited the shower stall and proceeded to where Melissa was sitting, which was by the prison's blue cell block doors. The doors were clearly locked for security measures but she quickly stood up when she noticed me standing there waiting. She gave me a sly look before she proceeded to unlock the door without taking her eyes off the sight of me.

"Finished?" she asked.

"Ya."

"You OK? You have been real quiet lately. What's cooking up in that head of yours?"

"Nothing at all. I'm just doing my time in peace," I said.

I was not interested in all the nice guy bullshit she was trying to portray now. Not after what I had to go through thus far. I had forgiven, but by no means would I forget.

"Well I am glad things got through to you. To just do your time and go home. Doesn't make sense fighting us. You will never win," she said with a conniving look on her face.

Little did she know, I had already won. The battle was not with them, it was with myself. I was my own worst enemy.

I followed Melissa through the Max unit, looking around to see if I noticed anyone. It was completely empty with not a guard in sight. It was like being lost in a deserted town. The feeling was off, and it kept getting stronger. Something was happening…something that did not meet my eyes. When I got back in my cell, I quickly searched for my sacred knife that I hid in my sock and thankfully it was still there. I checked the toilet to find out if the voice recorder was there and it was. It must have been my nerves because when I started getting ready, the feelings went away.

I could not wait to leave this place and smell the fresh, free air. To run wild and be free once again. To be able to walk freely amongst everyone else. My heart started beating at the anticipation and excitement. The thirstful taste for each breath. I could feel the wind blowing against my face. Watching the fall leaves change colours. I could see the beautiful patterns that the leaves made when changing seasons. Observing the everyday cycle of life in itself was amazing.

"BROWN!" Melissa shouted as she pounded on my cell unit.

"It's time?" I asked, trying not to appear eager.

"Yes, we are escorting you to the medical unit for your trip with Dr. Bakshi and Officer Pete." Did she just fucking say Officer Pete? Melissa handcuffed my hands from the other side of my prison cell door, and then proceeded to unlock it.

She escorted me and Ms. Jones, who totally ignored me when I looked at her to say hello. She kept her eyes to the floor and did not lift her head up once. As we made our way through the Max unit to enter into the compound, I noticed the women beginning their work days. Some raking leaves and others doing garbage duty to keep the prison clean. I did not notice any movement from House Five, but it was still early. As we made our way into the building, I heard my name.

"DIAMOND! Yo girl!"

It was Fatback. She was rushing her way up to me when Melissa blocked her from coming into contact by standing in front of me. The main building was empty except for the presence of Fatback. She did not do prison work. She was too busy muscling woman and getting high. Blonde and Fatback enjoyed the luxuries of being hustlers in prison. They did what they wanted when they wanted and no one could do shit about it, not even the Warden and she hated it.

"STOP RIGHT THERE!" Melissa said.

"Your girl Erica got out! She said she loves you and will write!"

My heart sunk as I was pushed on through the main building to the medical unit. She was the first woman I adored. The first love of my life. I did not know where she went or much about her, but my heart longed for her at that moment. I could see her pretty, grey, snow cat leopard eyes in the distance of my mind. She was unique and made me connect to a part of myself I never knew existed. She connected me to a love I have always yearned for. Screaming she loved me repeated in my mind. My eyes got teary and I had to clear my throat to hold back my agony. Ms. Jones turned around to look at me and our eyes made four.

"Alright inmates: handcuffs off and let's get you going," Melissa ordered.

"Why are we taking off the handcuffs?" I asked.

"Officer Pete has a new set of handcuffs strictly for the outside!"

"Oh," I responded, disappointed of course.

We entered the medical unit and there stood Dr. Bakshi with a smile, and Officer Pete with that dirty smirk on his face. He smiled at Ms. Jones who kept her eyes away from him.

"Let's get you all going! It's going to be a long morning ride as I've scheduled the appointments for this afternoon."

Officer Pete proceeded towards me and I stared down into his soul. He then moved his eyes in another direction as he locked up my handcuffs. When he made his way towards Ms. Jones she moved back as if she was in fear of him touching her at all. He noticed and got angry with her immediately.

"We don't have all day for your games, inmate Jones."

I looked at her and our eyes made four again. This time I blinked at her to let her know it was OK. I knew what Dr. Bakshi and I had planned. This Goddess would be free to wander the streets. She did not smile back or anything. She continued to look back down on the ground.

We exited the medical unit to freedom. Officer Pete had a beige Chevy Impala waiting in front of the exit to pick us up and transport us to the hospital. I tried not to smile, but I did not have a good poker face at all. The air that embraced my skin...I could taste freedom just a few miles away. It was mine.

CHAPTER FOURTEEN: Captivity

Well I'm just a soul whose intentions are good
Oh Lord please don't let me be misunderstood.
~Nina Simone

We arrived at the Grand River Hospital in Kitchener, Ontario. The drive was short but sweet. I could not wait to get out of the car. The awkward silence and the anticipation were tearing up at my insides. My stomach felt like it was on a roller coaster ride. The uneasiness travelling all through my body had made it hard to quiet my mind and just be. I looked over at Ms. Jones who was sleeping with her head rested on the back window. I don't know how she could sleep at a time like this. This was nerve racking no matter how hard I tried to ignore the emotions.

"Let's go ladies! There is no time like the present," Officer Pete muttered.

Ms. Jones jumped up from her sleep, laughing. She smiled at me as she was coming back to life, just like she did when we were in the showers. Officer Pete exited the vehicle first and opened both of our car doors. Dr. Bakshi already exited the car and was waiting for us. He assisted each of us out the car and unlocked the handcuffs to release us.

"Go with Dr. Bakshi. She will assist you from here."

I immediately thought to run, but I knew our plan was calculated. Ms. Jones jumped in the air repeatedly like a child as we followed Dr. Bakshi into the entrance doors of the Emergency Department at the hospital. She continued laughing while we trailed Dr. Bakshi down the corridors.

We continued down the left wing of the Grand River Hospital following the arrows behind Dr. Bakshi, when she stopped and turned around to speak to us.

"We don't have much time. There is a back door entrance just follow the arrows. I have a car coming to pick you both up. It is a good friend of mine. Diamond, please take care of Ms. Jones and don't leave her side. I am relying on you Diamond, as this is the moment you have prepared for."

"Thank you Dr…" I began to say before Dr. Bakshi interrupted.

"Don't thank me, just go and be safe! I will get to you very soon. When things die down," she said hurrying us along.

I grabbed Ms. Jones' hand and ran as fast as I could down through the hospital hallways to the exit. I had never run so fast in my life, but I knew what was at stake here. Ms. Jones who was silent now, ran just as fast. She was focused and knew we had to get out. We exited to the doors of freedom. The hospital doors slowly opened and there was no car in sight. I started to panic and looked at Ms. Jones; we both stood there in utter disbelief. My vision started to get blurry as the tears began to fill my eyes. Ms. Jones began pulling on my arm; when I looked up and noticed an Indian Sikh driver pull up in a Dodge Caravan. This had to be him. We smiled and ran to the car to get in. The driver looked at both of us long and hard, but did not unlock the door. He rolled down the window and spoke.

"You coming?" he asked.

"Yes!" I said with the biggest smile on my face.

He unlocked the door and we jumped in the black van. Just as he was about to pull out, five Kitchener police cruisers circled us.

"GET THE FUCK OUT THE VAN WITH YOUR HANDS UP!" the officer shouted from the first cruiser to arrive on scene.

A white-shirted, stocky officer with brown hair and blues eyes pointed his Glock 9 in our direction. I looked at the Indian man who was not in a panic at all; he smirked, fixing his orange Dastar.

"You must go," he said.

This all felt like a setup until I saw him reach for a black Mac-10 off his front car seat. I did not even notice it because it was hidden under a black towel.

"You must be going now! GET OUT!" he yelled at us. I sat for a moment and realized my breath of fresh air was short lived. We had a group of officers armed with their guns pointed at us, ordering us to come out the car. Crying was not the option right now. I looked at Ms. Jones and opened the van door. I exited first with my hands up and Ms. Jones followed right after. Two big white police officers rush towards us with their guns and tackled us down to the concrete ground.

"Why are you ladies riding with this crazy lunatic? Did you know he's on the run for the murders of thirty aboriginal women?" one officer said, but I could not see which one.

I lifted my head up and a car pulled up behind one of the cruisers. It was a white man with glasses. He looked right at me and kept driving along shortly after the officers let him through. They continued to order the Indian man out of the car but he did not budge. Ms. Jones and I were placed in the back of a cruiser.

"We will talk to you ladies down at the station, and we'll get your statements of what happened then."

"WAIT ONE MOMENT, OFFICER! THOSE ARE MY INMATES!" Officer Pete yelled as he came running towards us.

"I just called in a Canada wide warrant at the Kitchener PD for these two ladies. Trying to escape, were ya?"

Fuck my life. My heart sunk into my stomach and was about to fall out my ass.

"It's your lucky day, ladies! First you ride with a serial killing lunatic...on top of getting caught trying to escape from a federal prison," the short stocky officer said, laughing.

"Officer, follow me down to the station. I will press charges, and you can have these ladies back in your institution. Just got to place their handcuffs."

"GET DOWN! SHOTS FIRED! CODE RED! OFFICER DOWN! CALLING FOR BACK UP!"

The Indian serial killer had started shooting at the police to get away in his van. It was short lived, because they opened fire until the vehicle got stopped by slamming into one of the police cruisers. He looked like he was killed instantly because he was lifeless and had blood dripping down his face from a wound to the forehead.

Ms. Jones sat smiling with the biggest grin on her face like we were in an action movie. That's when she began to speak. "Thank you for the best day of my life. So much fun. I will never forget this day or you. You are much more than a Diamond. Your spirit lights all the dim lights around you."

I burst into tears and started bawling like a baby; all my emotions had finally surfaced and exploded all at once.

"OH SHUT UP WITH THE CRYING ALREADY! DON'T CRY NOW JUST BECAUSE YOU'VE BEEN CAUGHT!" the driving Officer said.

Everything was a blur to me. I started to lose my vision because of the tear drops that filled my eyes. I felt Ms. Jones trying to lean against me in comfort, but we were both handcuffed so we could not move our hands to touch each other. This was one of the most fucked up days of my life and Ms. Jones thought it was fun. I burst out laughing all while crying, and Ms. Jones joined me.

"SHUT IT UP! LOONEY ONE AND TWO BACK THERE!" the officer shouted as he gave us both a dirty look through his rear view mirror.

We continued laughing, enjoying our last moments of freedom.

CHAPTER FIFTEEN: Free

Expose yourself to the deepest fear; after that
fear has no power and the fear of freedom
shrinks and vanishes. You are free.
~Jim Morrison

After being booked and charged at the police station, we were brought back to the Grand Valley Institution for Women. We arrived to the whole prison of women cheering us on as we walked through the compound. They chanted:

"FTW! DBD!"

On repeat. Fuck the world! Death before dishonour! I smiled at Blonde and Fatback who were at the forefront of the pack of women cheering. I knew it was them who put this gathering together for our arrival. We quickly got escorted into the max unit by Officer Pete and Officer Jason.

The Max unit was exactly how we left it. Walls full of dead demon-filled secrets waiting to be told. I did not belong here. I could not belong here. Why had God put me back here? Or did I put myself back here? The questions flooded my mind as I entered my cell block unit in disbelief. Whatever was next to come, I could face it. Sitting down for a year or two more, on top of my sentence, was nothing. At least I would be trained, humbled, and ready to attack the outside world. The beast they had sit and let fester behind these walls, would be out one day. Fuck it! I tried and did not make it out. There must have been a reason. Maybe there was more to my story of experience that I needed to learn. Maybe it was a test of my faith.

I sat on my bunk for about an hour with thoughts and questions running all around in my head. What was next? Where was Dr. Bakshi? When was dinner coming? What time was it?

All my possessions had been taken out of my cell as a part of my punishment for escaping but I knew there was more coming. I knew the embarrassment these officers faced for having a prisoner escape—they would not let it slide. It was only a matter of time before they came for me and believe me I would need to be ready.

"COUNT!"

Speaking of the muthafuckin' devils. They didn't waste no time to arrive at my prison cell. I stood up to be counted but this count was strange. They did not open my unit or ask me to show my hands. They left me standing there waiting in silence until I decided to go sit down on my bunk.

"COUNT! AND IF YOU SIT DOWN WHEN IT'S COUNT AGAIN, YOU WILL BE CHARGED FIVE MORE YEARS MINIMUM ON TOP OF WHAT YOU'RE ALREADY GOING TO GET!" Officer Pete was fuckin' with me, and I knew this was just the start of his bullshit. Five years? This muthafucka must have been crazy if he thought they were going to add five years on to my shit. No matter how much meditation I did, I didn't know how humble I could be to face that. Twenty-three -hour lock up? Two-thousand one-hundred and ninety days or more? They must have been fuckin' crazy!

I stood there for count for a good five minutes in limbo when my prison door was opened. A huge bucket of ice water flew in my face. I tried to shield it but how the fuck do you shield water? The guards rushed right in after and pinned me to floor. Kicks, punches, and spit was all I felt all over my body.

"YOU GONNA LEARN, YOU LITTLE, DIRTY, BLACK BITCH! FUCKING COCKROACH! WE MAKE THE RULES HERE, AND YOU FUCKING ABIDE BY THEM!"

Officer Melissa was too happy to pay me back with a beating. She was too happy to see her revenge and my karma for what I did to her face. I laid there helpless on the concrete floor, with my mouth full of blood as I watched the only breath of air I would be inhaling as my prison cell block door closed. I slowly pulled myself off the floor and laid down on my bunk. All I could do was sleep. Sleep was my only escape.

"Please whatever I have done, please forgive me! I know you don't give us much more than we can handle but I'm not sure I can handle this for over two-thousand days! I don't know what I have done to deserve this but I'm willing to accept it. I give my soul to you. Whatever happens in this life, just know I did what I have learned and tried to change my ways for the better. I'm sorry for all the wrong I've done! Please forgive me. Amen," I chanted as my heavy, beaten up eyes closed to sleep.

"You will pay for what you've done," a soft male voice whispered in my ear. I tried to look around, but blackness was all I saw in the distance. I tried to get up but I was pushed back down. Was I dreaming? I tried to slap myself to wake up out of this dark nightmare but my hands were pushed down again.

"Don't fight, Diamond. Don't fight," Melissa the fat bitch whispered.

I tried to jump up with all the strength I had left in me, but the weight and strength was unbearable to fight. It was a man. I pushed up as hard as I could as the breaths of air were closing in. I had a mask or bag over my face and the weight of someone's body holding me down. I could not breathe. I continued trying to fight until something began to pull around my neck lifting my body up. I struggled trying to pull it off. I had no breaths left. I struggled to move but I couldn't; the suffocation of whatever was tied around my neck was taking the life out of me. I exhaled my last breath in agony as I watched my life on earth from birth flash before me. I began to see lights. Beautiful, exotic, warm, loving lights come toward me. I could hear the harmony of beautiful music that I had never heard before. It was a genre not explainable to mankind.

No! Not now! I thought. After a while the fight stopped and the lights sat watching. The pain I was feeling no longer existed. I was standing in my prison cell watching the three officers scramble around my cell. They were moving my limp, dead body into a plastic bag. I watched in love for I could see inside their souls. They were not the evil they portrayed to be. There is no such thing as evil or death. There is no judgment for we are one in the same. We are high vibrational souls having a human experience and we are not alone. There are many other forms and formless light lives that exist here in this universe.

I could see the whole prison. The prisoners and the officers, all one and the same. One light. One truth. One soul. We all are one. As above, so below. My journey was starting a new beginning. The life of mankind for me had ended, but the journey of light life had just begun. Higher dimension. Higher vibration. It was my time to be free.

LOVE IS...

What is it to be free?
Is it to physically walk
This earth without question?
The freedom to make
Choices of one's own right?
Is it the freedom to
Be who you are?
Is it having everything
Possible in your possession?
Is it escaping the mental
Shackles that have been
Placed upon your mind?
Is it death?
Does
Freedom come with a price?
Or is that life's answer?
Freedom faced me
The lights embraced me
All that was, was nothing
At all for I was released
From the bondage of mankind
All that I felt no longer existed
I felt the warmth of love
A love that was so unconditional
Forgiving and sacred
A love that did not need or want
For it is and will always
Be the answer to all
Love is freedom.

Thank you to all of you who participated in this series: to all who supported and enjoyed the books, and to all who made this possible for me to write to you.

One love!

*Always follow your dreams,
and don't let anyone tell you can't!*

*The world is yours and limits are endless.
~K. Haywood*

www.ingramcontent.com/pod-product-compliance
Lightning Source LLC
Chambersburg PA
CBHW031856170626
46807CB00004B/1756